Captured as a prisoner of war, Prince Clament expects rough treatment. However, the extent of torment he endures is beyond even his expectations. When Prince Braxton frees him, Clament knows it's only a farce meant to coerce him into finally spilling all his country's secrets. Except, despite all his efforts—magical and common—Clament finds himself helplessly drawn to Braxton, wishing he could believe the tantalizing promises Braxton makes.

Unfortunately, the war continues to be fought. When the ongoing battle spills into Clament's healing ward, resisting Braxton takes a backseat to simple survival. And yet, Clament knows he must make a terrible decision: believe in Braxton and betray his country, or betray Braxton and possibly get him killed. That is, assuming Clament is allowed to live long enough first.

THE PRINCE

PRINCES OF TOVAL, BOOK TWO

MELL EIGHT

A NineStar Press Publication
www.ninestarpress.com

The Prince

First Edition, January 2025

ISBN: 978-1-64890-794-4

Also available in eBook, ISBN: 978-1-64890-793-7

CONTENT WARNING:

This book contains depictions of graphic violence, mention of past sexual abuse of a minor character, attempted murder, mentions of torture.

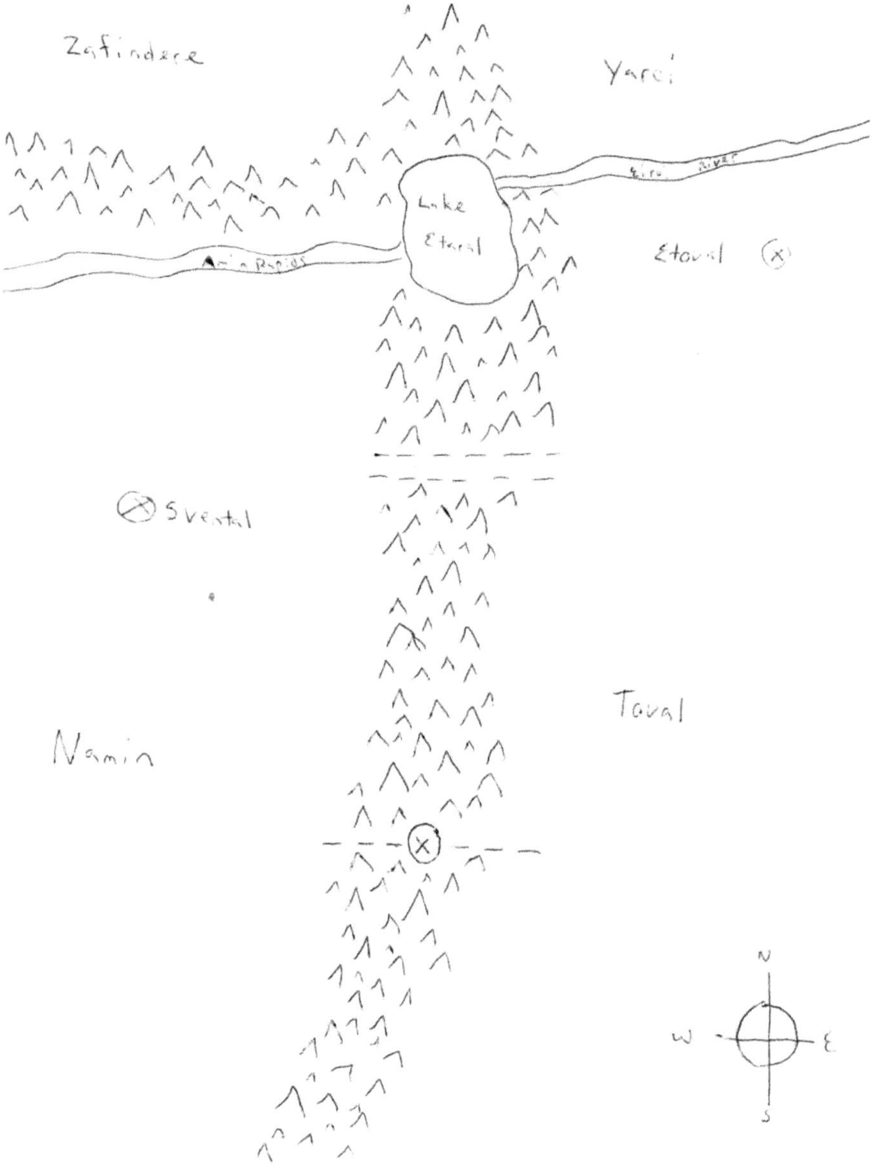

Zafindere
Yarei
Kire River
Lake Etaral
Amin Rapids
Etaval
Svental
Taval
Namin
N
W
E
S

Prologue

PRINCE CLAMENT OF the country of Namin walked through the campsite on the shores of Lake Estaral only half listening to the mercenary captain bitching in his ear about how long they had been left to wait with dwindling supplies. He tried to keep the sneer twisting his lips in place, but all he really wanted was to roll his eyes and go back to his own campsite where he could get some sleep. He really, really didn't want to be here.

The whole plot was a harebrained idea doomed to failure, but no one back in Namin had wanted to hear Clament's opinion. Instead, they had assigned him to lead these sorry excuses for mercenaries. The plan was simple: the mercenaries would descend from the Spikehorn Mountains into the lush northern farmland in the foothills less than a day's ride from here, where they would pillage the local villages into oblivion. The country of Toval, within whose borders those villages were located, would be forced to respond to protect their people by sending a large military contingent to repel the mercenaries. The military would be focused on rescuing the people and on rebuilding whatever was left of the villages. While Toval was distracted by what was happening in their north, Namin planned to invade in the south, using their forces to establish a new border where Namin could claim the land in those even lusher foothills.

There was no damned way such a moronic plan would work.

A glance around at the maybe two hundred mercenaries in the camp told Clament exactly how poorly the plan was going to go. Not a single mercenary had a properly maintained set of armor or weapons. Also, none of them would be particularly pleased with the idea of having to work together and split the spoils.

Assuming the mercenaries even agreed to participate—rather than just cutting their losses and heading out to find a better job—Clament knew what would actually happen. Should this ragtag group descend into Toval's northern farmland, the result was very likely going to be the exact opposite of Namin's grand, hairbrained plan: the mercenaries would attack and pillage the villages and Toval would respond. If Namin was lucky, Toval might send one full contingent of forces in response. A full contingent was probably overkill to defeat the mercenaries, if Clament was being honest. The rest of Toval's large and extremely well-trained army would remain in full readiness, completely able to respond to an incursion in the south.

Clament would probably be killed by Toval's forces in the battle, which, in hindsight, might explain why he was sent to lead the mercenary part of the plan. A convenient way of getting rid of him—having Toval remove his head. Clament would go from the hated bastard prince to a martyr killed by the great enemy of Toval, a dead figurehead used to unify the people of Namin under the king's call to arms. He was much more useful to Namin dead than alive, for this part of their grand plan, at least.

Two soldiers held open the flaps of the command tent as Clament ducked the low awning and stepped inside. The complaining mercenary captain followed, his mouth still running with yet more complaints. One by one the rest of the captains entered, each of them scowling and trying to look more intimidating than the others. Clament tried to out sneer them, in hopes that acting haughty would convince them to obey his orders. Last of all came the captain wearing the red patch on his piecemeal leather armor, denoting he was in charge of the Blood Lions. He ducked into the tent and looked up, immediately catching Clament's eyes.

Prince Fenwick of Toval, Commander of His Majesty's Royal Forces. Clament recognized him immediately.

And then all hell broke loose.

*

CLAMENT HADN'T BOTHERED counting the days since Toval had captured him; since Fenwick's pet chef had interfered and ruined the doomed-to-failure plot before it could even be implemented. Clament's hands were tied to the pommel of his horse's saddle, and his legs tied to the stirrups. One of the soldiers guarding him held the reins. Clament couldn't go anywhere. He couldn't even lift his hands to wipe away the deluge of rain dripping down his face.

They finally reached a fork in the road. The majority of the royal forces went left, while Clament and his cadre of guards took the righthand path. Not too much later, they arrived at a gate set into a thick wall. The momentary reprieve from the rain as they went through the long tunnel under the wall was the only good thing he could remember happening in a very long time. Unfortunately, they emerged into a courtyard soon after and the rain resumed.

The guards cut him free and hauled him down from the saddle, then they frog-marched him across the courtyard, two guards, one on each side, gripping Clament's arms. They walked for quite a few minutes, following the outside wall of what Clament wanted to assume was the palace of Etoval, the capital city of Toval and the royal seat, until they reached a nondescript door with a very heavy-looking lock. One of the guards banged on the door. Even over the dripping, pounding rain, the heavy *thunk* of a bar being removed, the rattle of a thick chain, and then the *thud* as the lock was turned was perfectly audible. Someone pushed the door open from the inside and his guards marched Clament into the building.

Clament dripped onto the gray flagstones for a few long seconds, taking in the narrow room. A sturdy chair sat off to one side, and the room was barely big enough for it. A second door with an equally large lock was across from the chair, and the guard who had opened the first door pounded on it.

Another *thunk, rattle, thud*, and the second door swung open, revealing yet another guard and a long flight of stairs heading downward. A third door that must be the access route directly from within the palace was to the left, but Clament's two guards took him down the stairs, which had two landings as it switched directions on the descent.

At the bottom was a dimly lit hallway of more gray flagstone floors. Six barred doors dotted the walls, three on each side. The guards took him to the farthest door on the right, pushing him inside and slamming the door shut behind him.

Clament was, thankfully, finally left alone. He reveled in the peace of it—of not being tied to another person when he wasn't tied to a horse—and took stock of his surroundings. The place wasn't cold, which was a small mercy since he left behind a puddle as he walked forward. A hard, wooden bedframe with a thin mattress and thinner blanket was set to the left, a hole in the floor in the back right corner was his latrine, and that was it. No window, no chairs, no obvious light fixtures. Nothing except the blanket and bed and pit.

Footsteps echoed down the hall. Clament turned to face the door, and a moment later, a new face appeared. Light brown hair and intense hazel eyes set in a face that would have been handsome if not for the stern scowl currently twisting his full lips—Prince Braxton of Toval, officially a captain in the palace guard, but Clament knew better. Braxton was the kingdom's spymaster and chief of all that happened in the dark and dank corners of the world. If he was here, it meant the king thought Clament had useful information, no doubt for their endless fight with Namin.

"You know who I am," Braxton began, his voice powerful but not too deep. He didn't mince words or try to pretend to be something he wasn't, or to be after something else. Clament respected that, even if it was in regard to the person on the other side of a barred and locked door. "You know what I want. Are you ready to talk?"

Clament only glared in response. He might not be liked by his family, but he wasn't a traitor. Braxton was going to have to wait a very long time to get any answers out of him.

"Very well," Braxton continued, shrugging. "I'll leave you to your thoughts for now, but I will return later. Perhaps you'll be in a better mood for talking then."

He left and blissful silence returned, but only momentarily. Enough time had passed for Braxton to have left the dungeon when Clament heard footsteps again. Two of the guards who had been with Braxton walked into view outside the bars, both of them grinning, their eyes shining with glee.

"You heard our dear prince," one of the guards said, his tone sing-song with happiness. He pulled out a key ring and unlocked the cell door, pushing it open and stepping inside before relocking the door behind him. "He wants you to talk. We're here to convince you." The smile grew and the guard clenched his fingers into a fist hard enough to make the knuckles crack.

Clament closed his eyes and let out a heavy sigh. So much for Braxton's veneer of civilization. Well, it wasn't like Clament hadn't been beaten before, and at least this guard didn't know all his weak points like his so-called brother. Still, Clament braced himself for what was to come. The best defense was offense, so he reopened his eyes and glared, hoping this wouldn't be too bad.

Interlude

Three Months Later

BRAXTON WALKED DOWN the last of the steps into the dungeons, stepping onto stone-flagged floors that were cheap, but easy to mop. Only political prisoners ended up in the palace dungeons; the prison complex for everyone else was about five miles north of the city, heavily fortified with specialty guards. Braxton didn't like going there, so it was nice Prince Clament was one of their pampered guests here in the palace. Braxton visited every couple of days to ask one simple question.

He walked down the hall, which had barred doors for six cells, three on either side, and stopped outside the last door on the right, peering through the bars at the lone person lying on the bed inside. Prince Clament had the blond hair and blue eyes of his entire family, the royal family of Namin. Normally, those brilliant blue eyes were glaring at the door, fierce and powerful and wonderfully defiant even with hair disheveled from months in a cell. This time, Clament was curled into a ball, huddled underneath the thin blanket.

"Are you ready to talk?" Braxton asked, his usual question feeling flat today.

Clament didn't answer, and Braxton could see he was shivering.

Braxton turned to one of the guards stationed in this wing. "Summon the healer," he ordered. The man dashed off, and Braxton turned to a second one. "Open this door."

The second man produced a key ring and fitted the key into the lock, which groaned as the lock was turned. The door hinges let out a screech as the guard yanked it open. And Clament didn't twitch.

Braxton hurried inside, his two personal guards following closely, and paused at Clament's side. He was definitely shivering, his nose curled up to his knees, and clutching at the blanket in clenched fists. Braxton slowly reached out, tentatively resting his palm against Clament's forehead and yanked his hand back with a hiss. Clament's skin was boiling.

"Why the hell am I back here so soon?" someone whined from the hallway. "I just put this bastard back together last night! Can't you wait a few days before ripping him to pieces?"

Braxton sucked in a sharp breath at the healer's words, clenching his own hands into fists to keep from lashing out. There was only one reason the healer would be familiar with this particular prisoner, a reason for which his words also implied. Braxton straightened and turned to face the door, catching both prison guards and the healer in his harsh, angry glare.

"Who signed the writ approving torturing this man?" Braxton asked, his voice eerily calm considering the fury churning inside, absolutely ready to explode like a volcano. "Answer me!" he roared.

"You wanted him to talk," the guard who had fetched the healer began, his voice a whine that had Braxton clenching his teeth and taking in slow breaths through his nose to keep from screaming again.

"The law is clear," he said, trying to sound reasonable and logical when all he really wanted to do was grab the guard and shake him until the stupid fell out. "Torture of political prisoners requires a royal writ, signed by the king or crown prince, and sealed by whichever one didn't sign. Tell me where you got a writ to touch this man?" Braxton prowled closer, and his two personal guards spread out to encircle the three men.

"You want answers, this is how you get them," the guard continued, still whining but sounding even more desperate as he glanced around the small space.

"Hands in the air. You're under arrest. All of you," Braxton added pointedly to the healer, who had opened his mouth to protest. The healer might not have participated in the torture, but he must have realized what was going on and done nothing to stop it. That made him equally guilty in Braxton's eyes.

Slowly, all three obeyed, although the loudmouthed guard and healer both looked like they wanted to argue. One of Braxton's guards, Mark, moved forward to disarm the two prison guards—he checked the healer, but he wasn't carrying anything—the other personal guard, Sapson, drew his sword and stood ready to intervene if needed. Braxton watched, arms crossed and scowling, seething inside.

How dare these mere guards presume to know what Braxton wanted! How dare they touch Clament! All the fire, his fierce beauty, now shuttered and hidden behind a thin blanket and high fever. And there was no telling what mental issues Clament bore since torture was more effective at breaking a man than getting actual answers.

"Luckily, we're already in a prison," Braxton said, bending down to retrieve one of the sets of keys on the ground next to the pile of weapons. He passed the keys to Mark. "Mark, put them each in their own cell. Quickly. I need to get Prince Clament to the healers' ward." He wasn't going to believe anything the healer down here had to say, not right now. The healers' ward had people Braxton knew he could trust.

Mark took the keys and dragged the three prisoners off, Sapson following, sword still at the ready. Braxton left them to it and turned to Clament. He gently slid his arms underneath the curled body, feeling the shivering rattle through his own bones, and picked Clament up. Clament's golden head rested against Braxton's shoulder, his puffing, panting breaths blowing against Braxton's neck. He walked out of the prison, heading for the secret passages that would keep Clament's presence and illness secret from gossipmongers and spies alike. Mark and Sapson caught up quickly, following as Braxton led the way through the passages to the healers' ward. Braxton walked as quickly as he dared, trying not to jostle Clament, and hoping he wasn't too late to save Clament's life.

Chapter One

HIS BODY'S SHIVERING knocked Clament out of what had been a rather pleasant dream of being curled against a warm chest, strong arms carrying him, and a comforting voice telling him it would be all right soon. He felt a bone-deep iciness, as if his actual bones had been replaced by icicles, and the shivering only made his frozen joints ache even more.

Clament clutched at the thick blankets on top of him, trying to wrap them tighter around himself to preserve some warmth. They didn't help. The cold was coming from within his body, not outside, so the barrier couldn't stop the cold. At least the blankets were plentiful and the mattress underneath him soft; he could attempt to derive some comfort from that.

Except… Clement forced his eyes open, looking blearily around at his surroundings. The white walls wobbled as he shook, and the space slowly spun around him too, but it was definitely not a prison cell. He shut his eyes again before he added nausea to the cold he was feeling, but at least his brain was engaged and whirring again.

He was clearly very ill. Perhaps being captured and tortured was all a terrible fever dream? But that couldn't be it. He remembered starting to feel bad after the healer had finished with him a few sessions ago, an odd tightness to his lungs and a slow cough that said something wasn't right. Which meant he must still be in Etoval, but that didn't explain why he wasn't in the dungeons. Prisoners didn't get soft blankets and mattresses, even if they were princes.

The click as the door opened seemed loud in the room, and Clament tensed instinctively, his body curled to protect his vulnerable stomach. Soft footsteps clicked closer, as if whoever had entered the room and was approaching Clament was trying to be quiet. Even despite his body's constant shivering, Clament was ready for whatever was about to be inflicted on him. A moment later, soothing warmth filtered through his body rather than sharp pain, and Clament risked opening his eyes again, surprised and anxious to figure out what was going on.

The woman standing at the side of the bed was wearing a light green tunic over brown pants. Green light glowed around her hands, which she held about an inch over Clament's blanket-covered body.

"How is he?" a familiar voice asked quietly. Clament thought it sounded like Braxton, but Braxton had never before sounded so gentle and meek. When he showed up at the prison to question Clament, he presented the picture of a man certain in his skin, one who was always confident and aggressive in getting what he wanted. Braxton had to have been the man who had ordered Clament's torture, but then had him all healed up so he wouldn't have to see the ugly parts of what breaking a man like Clament entailed.

"He is healing surprisingly well, considering, Your Highness," the healer replied. "As you know, the pneumonia was really advanced, with significant damage to his lungs. I have repaired the worst of it, so his lungs are almost cleared of the fluid buildup, but he still has quite a ways to go. I exhausted a lot of his energy while I was healing him, plus his muscles were somewhat starved of oxygen, so I expect him to feel weakness in his limbs for a few weeks, if not months. The poor boy is going to have a very a long recovery ahead of him. The problem right now is reducing this stubborn fever so we can get him started in that direction."

"You're the best healer in this palace, Alina," Braxton said, his tone half joking, half serious. "I know you can help him feel better."

"I'll certainly try," she answered, the green glow intensifying.

More soothing warmth filtered deep into Clament, cracking some of the ice surrounding his bones. The feeling was so comforting. No matter how badly he wanted to stay aware when Braxton was in the room, Clament's eyes slid closed and his mind drifted off, sleep taking him away.

Waking a second time was better. He was still tucked beneath thick blankets, on an incredibly comfortable mattress in the white room. He wasn't shivering, though, which made for a very nice change. Instead, he felt completely worn out as if he hadn't slept for a week, coupled with doing multiple stints in the gladiator's ring. Namin's national sport was fighting, and the ring was the grandest place to show off the best of the best. Clament would never come close to being good, let alone the best, at any kind of fighting. He was passable with a sword, although Prince Fenwick had handily beaten him there. He knew how to hand fight and wrestle, but he wouldn't want to test his abilities. Clament's skills had always leaned toward his ability to reason—he knew he could outthink every one of his family members—but that wasn't something that impressed in Namin. Brawn always beat brains. Yet another reason for his so-called family to despise him. And apparently, he also felt nasty enough for his thoughts to go morose. Clament let out a huff of air and carefully pushed the blankets away. He sat up slowly, waiting for the moment of inevitable ache. Except, it didn't come. He didn't feel up to actually getting out of bed, but at least he could look around.

White walls. White ceiling. White blankets on a white bed. Even the floors were pale gray that did nothing to break up the stark unpleasantness of the room. The wall to his right had a tall cabinet, also white, and aside from the bed, that was it for furniture. The opposite wall had a window covered with an opaque white shade that blocked the light so Clament couldn't guess the time or even whether it was day or night. He had no idea how long he had been here rather than in his cell.

The door clicked as the handle turned, cutting Clament's swirling thoughts short as a spike of adrenaline shot up his spine and his heart rate accelerated. He turned to look, trying to school his features into a bland expression to conceal the fact that a moment ago he had been wide-eyed with fear at the idea of someone approaching. Thankfully, only the female healer from before stepped into the room. She smiled when she saw he was up.

"There you are," she said, still smiling. "Glad to see you're feeling better. Terrible what happened to you."

Clament swallowed, trying to push back the feeling that his heart was beating in his throat. She seemed harmless, and Clament's experience with healers—albeit admittedly limited—was that they didn't inflict additional pain on their patients.

"The orders of a royal prince…" Clament forced out with a fatalistic shrug, trying to seem nonchalant about it all. She might be a healer, but she was still in the employ of Prince Braxton. Clament couldn't afford to come across weaker than he already did. Except, she adamantly shook her head in response, making him blink in surprise.

"That's the most terrible part of it, or so I've heard." She tapped the side of her nose. "The main guard who tortured you was executed," she whispered, her tone full of horror. "The second guard and the healer who failed so spectacularly at patching you back up both got life sentences. And Prince Braxton delivered the orders in court himself. He was that furious."

Furious Clament had gotten so ill Braxton had needed to pause his ministrations and make what he was doing to Clament public knowledge, no doubt.

"Never fear though," she continued, not noticing the direction of his scornful thoughts. "I'm the best healer here in Toval, remanded to the royal family almost exclusively. Prince Braxton was most insistent. I'll have you fixed right up in no time," she finished, grinning at him.

Which meant, of course, in only a short period of time Clament would find himself back in that dungeon under a more capable torturer's care. Well, at least he had a little longer to enjoy a comfortable bed and warm blankets. The last time he had slept in a real bed had been well before his assignment at Lake Estaral which had been a rather long time ago. Clament didn't actually know how long had passed since his capture. Weeks, probably months, but his torturers hadn't come every day, nor had Braxton, so he couldn't count the days by their appearances. His cell hadn't had a window either. He was certain his healer had been instructed not to answer any of his questions, so Clament didn't bother asking.

"I appreciate your help," he said instead.

"Oh! Where are my manners!" she gasped. She stepped back and executed a perfect curtsy. "Healer Alina, at your service. A pleasure to meet you."

Clament bowed from the waist, not certain he could stand long enough to give a proper reply. "I can't say it's a pleasure to make your acquaintance, Healer Alina, but I appreciate your help."

She giggled at his cheekiness as she stood straight again. "No, I suppose you wouldn't be. Anyway, now you're awake, I suspect you'll be wanting some food. Prince Fenwick's personal chef sent over some chicken broth for you. Said it would help heal you even more than my magic, and I have to agree. I tasted it, and it's like drinking liquid gold. I swear." She tapped two fingers to her heart in the sign for a heart's promise. "Be right back."

She scurried from the room, leaving Clament trying to hide a frown. Fenwick's personal chef was probably the man with blue cooking magic who had saved Fenwick when Clament had been following through on his orders to kill anyone who might interfere with the grand plan—such that it was. Clament had seen the way Fenwick looked at his chef, and the way the chef had looked back. The chance the chicken broth was poisoned was very high, and Clament knew he would have to eat it. Alina seemed to think he was safe here, but he knew better. He very much knew better.

She puttered back into the room before Clament had steeled himself and gently deposited a tray in his lap. Below the cloche was a cereal bowl full of clear, yellow broth and a spoon. A small glass full of orange juice was next to the bowl.

Clament tried to swallow back his nerves, but his mouth was

completely dry. Still, it was better to get it over with. He picked up the spoon and dipped it into the broth, blew on it for a second to cool it, and then stuck the full spoon into his mouth.

Liquid gold was an apt description. Deeply flavorful, nuanced with hints of the vegetables, chicken, and spices that had boiled together for hours to create such a glorious taste. Yet it was still mellow and easy for his fever-weakened body to handle. Another spoonful arrived in his mouth, as if his hand were autonomous from his brain. If the broth was poisoned, it was worth dying while eating this.

Clament almost felt like crying when his bowl was empty, but he felt full and rather sleepy, so he didn't ask for more.

The juice was tart and definitely didn't go with the soup, but there were different vitamins in the juice, so he understood why Alina waited until he finished that before she whisked the tray away again.

He yawned when she returned, which made her cluck. With her help, he was able to lie back down. Alina tucked the covers around him, but as Clament's head sank into the depths of his pillow, sleep swept him away.

Chapter Two

SURPRISE WAS THE first emotion Clament felt as he swam back to consciousness. He wasn't shivering uncontrollably again, nor was he sweating through his clothes. No sharp pains, jittery limbs, or fuzzy vision. All of which meant he hadn't been poisoned, which made absolutely zero sense. The perfect opportunity for a bit of revenge, and Prince Fenwick's chef had let it slip on by, untaken? If they were in Namin, Clament would have been poisoned multiple times already. Clament had a small amount of immunity to most poisons, given how many times he had survived such attempts. But then, he wasn't in Namin anymore. Toval was a completely different place, with a completely different ethos. Or so he had been taught—often by Namese teachers with incredible scorn in their voices. Braxton torturing him was completely in line with Clament's Namin-born expectations; that chef not poisoning him must be an exception to the rule.

A rustle of paper to his left made him stiffen in surprise. Clament slowly turned his head to look and frowned. The sorriest excuse for a desk he had ever seen had been added to the room. The surface was barely large enough to hold the two stacks of paper and single pen on top. Curled awkwardly behind it on a chair was Braxton, scowling fiercely at whatever was on the paper in his hand and paying no attention to Clament.

Clament gaped at Braxton for a long moment, trying to come up with any explanation as to why Braxton was in Clament's room and had chosen to do his work in such a ridiculous manner. No doubt Braxton had a grandly appointed office somewhere else in the palace yet for some reason, he was enduring uncomfortable conditions at Clament's bedside. None of it made any sense to Clament. Well, boggling over Braxton's actions wasn't going to get him any answers, Clament decided as he clenched his jaw and steeled his nerve. The only way to find out was to ask.

Despite his determination, he had to swallow twice to wet his throat before he found the courage to let Braxton know he was awake. Clament forced the appropriate amount of scorn into his tone, hoping to hide the fact that his hands were shaking and gut roiling beneath the cover of the blankets.

"Ask your damned question, and then go away," he said as he slowly sat up.

Braxton jumped, slamming his knee into one corner of the desk and then scrambling to catch one of the piles of papers as it listed dangerously.

"You're awake!" he gasped. "How are you feeling? Wait—" He waved one hand through the air between them as if clearing the space. "No, I need to start again." He walked out from behind the desk to stand at Clament's bedside and suddenly bowed deeply at the waist. "I am so, so, so damned sorry. I know that's not enough, just saying that, but apologizing is all I can do."

He straightened and a zing of horror rang through Clament at the sight of Braxton's eyes, damp and remorseful—and also incredibly pretty when they were soft like that. But, no. Clament forced that thought away as quickly as it had slithered in.

"Torture requires a royal writ," Braxton continued, "signed by the king or heir and sealed by the other and has not been approved in approximately three decades. I cannot order it on my own, and the guards are aware they must have a notarized copy of the writ before they can engage in such base practices. I promise, no writ was drafted, let alone approved for what was done to you, and my inattention allowed you to be heinously hurt for three long months." He paused to let out a heavy breath. Braxton squeezed his eyes shut as if he was trying to force the tears back, but when he opened them again, they were still alluringly soft and wistful. "Apologizing isn't enough, I know. You should be aware that you are welcome to stay here as long as you need to heal and are free to leave whenever you wish. I would be happy to arrange personal escort to the Namin border, or to wherever you prefer to go. Just let me know."

Braxton had to be bluffing. That was the only explanation Clament could come up with. As spymaster, he was likely an excellent actor who could produce tears on cue. Torture and confinement hadn't worked—had almost killed Clament without Braxton obtaining any intelligence out of him—so now Braxton was clearly trying the carrot instead of the stick.

Clament would play along for as long as he could draw out being treated nicely. Good food, a comfortable bed, a real healer instead of a quack; Clament would enjoy the privileges for as long as they lasted, secure in the knowledge that Braxton was only offering the comforts in order to drag information out of him.

"Healer Alina told me the people who…" he trailed off, unsure how to say tore him apart and patched him back together while being politically correct. And also without shuddering as the memories tried to resurface. Clament forced them back down, barely, the echo of his screams resounding in his head for only a brief moment before he was able to make them go away—to stuff all the bad things back down into a box with a secure lid covered in padlocked chains.

"They have been tried, convicted, and their sentences imposed," Braxton stated, his voice a dark growl filling the silent hole Clament had left by not speaking. "Whom they hurt was kept confidential, but they were made a public example to ensure something like that never happens in Toval again." His fingers flexed as if in his remembered anger he wanted to wrap his hands around those guards' necks.

Braxton really was an amazing actor. Or, perhaps, this anger wasn't feigned. Those guards had allowed Clament to get too sick to continue torturing, probably ruining whatever plans Braxton had concocted.

Braxton sighed and shook his head, his hands relaxing back to his sides. "I should leave you to your rest. Can I get you anything?"

Clament should have expected that question, but his jaw still dropped for a moment before he clicked his teeth shut again. Braxton was clearly leaning hard into the carrot option, which meant Clament had an opportunity to see how far the act would go. What was something he could ask for that would require real effort on Braxton's part but wouldn't push the envelope too far into prematurely ending the façade? A glance around the very white room gave him an idea.

"Can you do something to make the view a little less stark?" he asked.

If he was going to be living here for a while as he healed—as Braxton had implied—asking for something to look at wasn't ridiculous, but also required Braxton to find and organize bringing it here.

Braxton glanced around as well, chuckled, and nodded. "I'm sure I can find something." He returned to his awkward desk and gathered the stacks of papers. "I'll send Alina in to check on you, but I'll be back again soon."

Braxton paused by the door and looked back at Clament, his gaze searching as if he needed to reassure himself that Clament was starting to feel better. A flash of heat sizzled through Clament's body, rushing from his toes to the tips of his hair, and he ducked his head to hide his blush, cursing inwardly because he had zero idea why his body was reacting so inappropriately. A glance up through his eyelashes revealed Braxton's expression suddenly soften, the slightest upturn lifting his lips in a smile, before his usual stern expression resurfaced and he left the room. The door shut softly behind him, but there was no telltale click of a lock engaging.

Something was clearly wrong with Clament. His dry mouth and shaking hands could possibly still be caused by fear, yet the way his heart was thumping said otherwise. That strong, commanding gaze, brightly intelligent while still showing a soft and gentle mien, just plain did it for him. He had to find a way to dispel such ridiculousness. Braxton was the man who had ordered him tortured, who no doubt reveled in the game he was now playing to extract information from him, and Clament was acting like a teenager with a crush. Even mentally, the last part of that thought was full of scorn.

Luckily, there was a way for Clament to find out what Braxton was really up to. He closed his eyes to reduce the distortion of seeing two places at once and called on his magic. Gold light flared—the color of royal magic—and he relaxed against the headboard as he thrust his vision through the door and into the room just beyond where Braxton was talking with Alina.

"Really does look significantly better," Braxton was saying as Clament's magic got him close enough to overhear the conversation in progress. "Your healing powers are far too impressive for you to be stuck here in our tiny kingdom. You should be out in the world, making millions in gold and jewels."

"And never be able to have the face-to-face contact with my patients, or get to know the people I'm working with on a personal level," Alina cut in, frowning at Braxton. "I like where I am just fine. Your prince was a challenge to heal—his lungs were significantly damaged by the time he reached my ward—but I've managed to patch him up. He'll be a few more weeks on total bedrest though."

"Damn." Braxton hissed out a breath through his teeth. "The punishment the court handed down on those guards wasn't nearly enough." He shook his head. "Well, we should do something to keep him from going stir-crazy. I'll have a librarian come by with a selection of books, and I'll inform the head servant to make that room look less like a healing ward. Will you keep him company when you're not busy?"

Alina smiled. "Of course. He's a lovely young man. If he's awake, I'll get him some food. I had to find a lock to put on the pot of broth Char sent over, you know. Too many people just wanting to have a taste, and I almost ran out!" She laughed. "Speaking of someone completely overqualified for his position."

"Yes, well, like you, Char is happy. And Fen is happy too." Braxton shrugged. "In the end, that's all that really matters." A woman in what Clament guessed was a secretary's uniform dashed into the room, arrowing straight for Braxton. "Duty calls," Braxton said, sighing. "Thanks, Alina."

"Of course." She waved him off and headed to the far side of the room as Braxton followed the secretary out the double doors.

Clament wanted to follow Braxton, but the gentle tug between his eyebrows said he had better not. He was overextending, and his weak body couldn't handle the strain using his magic caused. He floated back to his body and opened his eyes, the golden glow dissipating as he mulled over what he had just seen.

No mention of poison, or of a plot. Of course, Braxton wouldn't tell her if Alina was innocent, but the way Braxton had appeared so concerned about Clament's comfort seemed a little too much for mere acting. Braxton had to be up to something. Clament knew that. And yet, a part of him wanted to believe Braxton was telling the truth. Since that was the same part that sighed ridiculously over Braxton's pretty eyes, Clament forced that thought aside. Braxton was no doubt waiting for Clament to relax his guard, to start believing in Braxton, and then the prying questions would start as he used the carrot to dig for information.

Too bad for Braxton that Clament wasn't going to be that easy to fool. Clament's family were masters at that very slimy craft; Braxton's attempts were going to be feeble in comparison.

Clament smoothed the soft blankets over his lap and let out a heavy breath. Like he had thought before: he would enjoy the comforts while they lasted, braced and ready for when it all vanished again.

Chapter Three

CLAMENT FOUND HIS bookmark as a knock sounded on the door.

"Enter!" he called. A moment later, the door opened and Braxton stepped into the room.

Clament slid his bookmark into place and shut the book, setting it aside on the small table next to his bed. The table's rich, dark wood complemented the green sheets on his bed and the patchwork quilt in deep reds and purples made from velvet and weighted silk cloth cut in different-sized squares and rectangles.

The rest of the room was just as fancy. Over the last two weeks, the items with color had slowly trickled in. A small tapestry hung next to the door, a green meadow dotted with red and purple flowers that matched his quilt. The window shades were a gauzy fabric in light green, covering the more generic, white, light-blocking ones original to the room, which hung underneath. A deep purple rug filled the floor between the bed and windows. The look was garish and not what Clament would have chosen for himself, but eons better than the painfully stark white.

If he had an informal parlor here, Clament would consider commandeering the quilt to use as a throw blanket for the couch. He didn't particularly care for the rest of the furniture, but the quilt was definitely growing on him. Back home in Namin, he only had a small room and attached bath at the castle, which he only saw maybe a handful of times a year. He was always being sent out on one mission or another—often in the hopes he wouldn't return, he thought—and his failure at this latest mission likely meant he wouldn't see his room again. Of course, it wasn't as if Clament actually enjoyed spending any time in the castle. Even when he tried to hide in the alleged sanctuary of his private bedroom, his father and brother could find him readily.

Somehow his room in the healers' ward, as garish as it was, came across far more welcoming than his room in Namin. Plus, his only visitors were Braxton and Alina, and he liked Alina despite all his mental admonitions. She legitimately seemed to care only about helping him heal; she had no ulterior motives and had never come across as if she knew she was only healing him so he would be strong enough to endure the next round of torture when it arrived.

Braxton, on the other hand… Clament let out a soft sigh.

"Good afternoon, Your Highness," Clament said.

"Hey," Braxton replied, one of his blindingly brilliant, far too beautiful for Clament's resolve smiles breaking across his face. "How are you feeling today?" He settled into the chair next to the too-small desk now pushed back against the wall. Braxton didn't visit every day, and the amount of time he could stay differed, but he did come by regularly. Sometimes he brought a stack of papers and hunkered down at that desk for an hour or two while Clament read, but most of the time was like today, where he could only stop by for a few minutes to say hello before his duties dragged him off again.

"Not much different than yesterday," Clament explained, shrugging. "Alina said she would be by soon to help me take another short walk to build back my strength. My lungs are as strong as they're going to get with magic; they just need time to heal at this point. And all of my other wounds are better." Clament had said basically the same thing yesterday and the day before, but despite that, Braxton's smile took on a relieved edge as if he had let out a pent-up breath and relaxed slightly.

"Good to hear. I can't stay long today, unfortunately. I wanted to let you know I have to leave the city for a few days. I should be back by Moonsday. If you need anything while I'm gone, please tell Alina. I've instructed my siblings to help you while I'm away, and she can contact them for you."

More likely, he had instructed his siblings to keep an eye on Clament to make sure he didn't do anything squirrely—which Clament firmly believed was the real reason why Braxton visited regularly—but it was good to know Clament wasn't being handed off to some army stooge or one of Braxton's subordinates in whatever clandestine business he ran for Toval.

In some ways, Clament enjoyed Braxton's visits. Only in the small, hidden part of himself he was vehemently suppressing, of course, but the warmth Braxton exuded—even if it was feigned as part of his act—was addicting.

"Safe travels," Clament responded, giving Braxton a small smile in return.

"Thanks." Braxton stood and started walking to the door, but paused awkwardly to look back at Clament as if he wanted to say something more. His mouth opened, then closed again, and he gripped the handle and pulled the door open. "I'll see you on Moonsday," he finally said before leaving and shutting the door firmly behind him.

"See you," Clament echoed into the empty room, wondering what that was about. Part of Braxton's act? A mistake in his act or failure of his acting skills? Or was Braxton genuine? Clament dashed that last thought away with a mental scoff. Whatever Braxton was up to, Clament refused to fall victim to it.

Not willing to dwell on it, Clament returned to his book, settling in until Alina came by to help him get some exercise a few hours later. He tried to get lost in the novel, but his brain was churning, thoughts swirling on wondering where Braxton was going and why. The spymaster of Toval had people come to him or sent out minions to gather information from his people in the field. There was no reason for him to travel somewhere unless whatever he was up to was so incredibly sensitive Braxton couldn't trust it to anyone else. Which, of course, no doubt meant Namin was up to something again.

Clament let out a sigh, forcing himself to focus on his book. Worrying about his father scheming was like worrying water was wet. Father schemed and plotted and distrusted everyone constantly, and his biggest target when Clament wasn't around was Toval.

What if he told Braxton about the plot to take over the southern farms in Toval? The traitorous thought slipped out before Clament could suppress it. Still, the plot was dead at this point since his role as a distraction in the north had failed so miserably. Would telling Braxton hurt anything more than his pride? Certainly it would end the painful status quo they were stuck in, where Braxton pretended to be offering a carrot since the stick hadn't worked and Clament pretended he didn't know what Braxton was doing. Ending the façade would almost be a relief, since Clament would finally know where he stood.

Of course, then it would be back to the prison and an end to all this luxury. Yet, at the same time, it would also mean an end to waiting for the other shoe to drop. Was losing his access to comfort worth stopping the constant anxiety? Clament didn't know.

Clament growled to himself, disgusted with both his indecision and the fact that he was even considering betraying Namin. The answer was no; he could not tell Braxton anything. He could not let Braxton win their little game.

Resolute—or at least pretending to be—Clament picked his book up again and this time it swept him away.

He looked up again when there was another knock on the door. This time, Alina walked into the room, holding a tray with a steaming teapot, a delicate china cup, and a rocks glass full of about a finger's width of the murky-green-colored, opaque, and bitter liquid masquerading as medicine that Alina had him taking every afternoon. The shadows on the floor cast by the sun through the windows said quite a few hours had gone by since Braxton had stopped in. Braxton was likely well on his way to whatever task he was journeying to, but Clament firmly yanked his thoughts back to Alina and the green goop. He didn't need to worry about what Braxton was doing and whether he would be okay, or how dangerous the assignment he was on that the Prince Spymaster had to attend to it personally. *No*, Clament scolded himself. He had already banished those same thoughts once. All he needed to worry about right now was forcing that noxious green sludge down without throwing it up again.

"I brought you tea to help wash it down," Alina said, correctly guessing what half of Clament's grimace was about.

"You think tea is going to cover up the taste of that slime?" he asked, whining slightly because he knew it would make her smile.

She laughed. "It won't hurt. Your daily dose of slime is why you're already walking. The sooner you drink it, the sooner we can go get that exercise."

"Fine, fine." Clament made a production out of sighing heavily as he reluctantly reached for the glass as she held the tray out toward him, his behavior only half feigned. His fingers touched the side of the glass, and then he stopped, freezing in place as an odd sort of tingling swept through his awareness. His magic roiled, the slightest bit of gold shining out of his eyes. Someone with ill-minded intent toward Clament had just stepped into his magic's passive field of awareness. Which meant somewhere nearby, inside the castle, someone was preparing to kill him.

Chapter Four

"WE NEED TO evacuate the healing ward," Clament said, throwing his blankets back. He got his legs over the side of the bed and stood, wobbling, but he refused to fall. His knees stabilized, and he headed for the door.

"What? Why? Where do you think you're going?" Alina gasped out.

Clament didn't know if he had time to explain, but he also knew he needed Alina's help to get everyone who might be in the healing ward to safety. He called up his magic, the room taking on a gentle golden glow.

"Sorry about this," Clament said as he clamped one hand on Alina's arm and dragged her awareness away with his, along the path his magic carved through the castle. They stopped in what appeared to be a dusty, unused storeroom where five people crouched. They wore dark, nondescript oversized clothes over leather armor, hoods over their heads, and masks covering their noses and mouths. The strip of skin around their eyes was darkened by some sort of powder.

"Shouldn't we wait till dark?" a woman asked, her voice a hissing whisper.

"Guards expect danger to happen at night," a man hissed back. "Our source says the damned princely guard dog is gone, and this is the time of day when the ward he's in is emptiest. We'll be able to get in, kill the bastard, remove any witnesses, and get out before anyone notices. Prepare yourselves."

Leather creaked as armored bodies moved and hands were placed on sword hilts. Clament let the magic go, returning to his body with a gasp echoed by Alina's.

"Where can we hide?" Clament asked.

Alina dropped the tray onto the end of the bed, green goop and tea splashing onto the lacquered wood, and dashed ahead of him into the main ward. Clament usually took his walks around the wide room, so the octagonal space was familiar. Two rows of beds down the middle for short-term treatment, four doors on the back wall leading to private treatment rooms—including Clament's—two more doors on each side, the left leading to storage and the right to the herbarium where concoctions like the green goop were made. The rest of the walls were absolutely stuffed with cabinets, except for directly ahead where wide double doors were open to the hallway outside.

"Marcia, get Lord Loweseth up. The ward is about to be attacked," Alina called to a young woman in trainee robes, sitting idly in a chair by the door.

Marcia gaped for a moment before swallowing hard and jumping to her feet. She hurried over to the only occupied bed in the middle of the room and gently shook the shoulder of the young man sleeping there, one of his arms immobilized in a sling. Alina went over to one of the cabinets and yanked the door open, revealing a staircase partially obscured by the healer's robes hanging inside.

Every inch of space was needed in the ward, so the healers had hung the robes there out of necessity, inadvertently converting a hallway concealed by a doorway into an actual secret passage. Alina pushed the robes to the side, holding them back and waving for Clament, Marcia, and Loweseth to start up the stairs. She closed the door after them and rearranged the robes so they filled the entire space, making it look like a proper closet. It would only hold up to a cursory inspection but would buy them some time.

Clament's knees were shaking, and he was gripping the banister with both hands to haul his body up by the time he reached the top of the stairs. Marcia helped Loweseth, whose eyes were unfocused and blinking out of sync, and Alina brought up the rear. She hurried forward to guide Clament to one of the chairs arranged in a long row on a balcony overlooking a circular room below.

"This is the observation room into the surgery," she explained.

A massive crashing noise echoed up the stairs from behind them. Alina let out a squeaking gasp and dashed over to the wall where a number of bellpulls were strung. She gripped the pull with a red string and yanked it frantically for a good thirty seconds before returning to Clament's side.

"That will summon the guards," she explained. "Come on. We have to keep moving."

Marcia hadn't stopped, so she and Loweseth were halfway down the stairs to the operating theater below by the time Alina levered Clament back to his feet. More of his weight than Clament really wanted to admit rested on Alina as she steadied him with an arm around his waist, his arm over her shoulders. Together they hobbled after Marcia, slowly making their way first to the staircase, and then step-by-step down. They were stumbling their way across the theater floor around the surgery bed and equipment in the center, when another loud crash sounded, and voices began to echo from above. The attackers had found the hidden staircase, which meant in moments he and Alina would be exposed to attack from above.

Clament bit his lip and pushed his legs to a faster pace, his lungs burning as he wheezed for breath. The open doors to the hallway loomed ahead, Marcia and Loweseth already through. Clament and Alina dashed out the doors, right into a group of six soldiers. Clament reeled back, almost knocking himself and Alina over, before he recognized the uniform of the Etoval palace guards.

"Attacking the ward!" Marcia was in the midst of speaking, and he realized she was informing the guards.

"How many attackers? Any hostages?" the man with a captain's stripes across his chest asked.

"Five attackers. No hostages. We got everyone out," Alina replied. "But they're right behind us."

The captain nodded sharply. He pointed at one of the six soldiers with him. "Sprint back to the guards' room and get everyone there down here immediately." The guard took off. The captain pointed to another soldier, a large woman with more muscles than the rest of the guards combined, and then pointed down the hall where the infirmary doors were visible. "Guard the doors. No one comes out. When reinforcements arrive, go in and clear the space, then come through the operating room to flank the bastards from behind. Capture if you can, kill if there's no other option."

The woman nodded and trotted off, sword drawn. The captain turned to the remaining four soldiers. "With me."

They drew their swords and marched into the operating theater, but Alina headed off, farther down the hall where she could tuck Clament onto a bench in a convenient niche. He couldn't watch through the doors from there, although Clament wasn't certain he actually wanted to know what was about to happen. A moment later, the sounds of battle echoed into the hallway: metallic clangs of blades clashing, grunts and shouts, and moans of pain. A full minute passed and then the thumps of boots stomping on flagstones preceded a dozen guards dashing into view, Prince Fenwick leading.

Prince Fenwick didn't slow as he passed Clament, although he shot what appeared to be a relieved nod in his direction. Clament must have imagined it, though, because there was no way the prince who had captured him would be relieved he was still alive. Half the group continued down the hall to the waiting guard outside the infirmary doors. The rest were with Fenwick as they all drew swords and headed inside the operating theater.

The battle didn't last long after that. Fenwick returned, looking disgruntled, his sword sheathed at his hip.

"They killed themselves when they saw they were outnumbered," he explained. "Poison hidden in a false tooth. I've seen it before." He snorted in disgust.

"Any of ours wounded?" Alina asked.

"Scrapes and bruises, Healer, but you're welcome to go check yourself. I'll keep an eye on your patients for you."

Alina stood and dusted off the seat of her pants before pointing at Loweseth. "That one was thrown from his horse this morning and has a broken collarbone. Don't let him thrash about. Make sure this one"—she moved her finger to point at Clament—"is still breathing." She waved for Marcia to follow, and they both vanished back through the doors into the operating theater.

Fenwick glanced at where Loweseth was lying on the floor, clearly still doped up on painkillers and insensible, and then leaned against the wall and switched his attention to study Clament.

"They say the king of Namin is the 'great all-seeing ruler' or the 'all-knowing king.'" The grin Fenwick leveled on Clament was full of mischief, his hazel eyes twinkling in the light of the dim, windowless hallway. "Let's just say I have some inkling of how everyone managed to evacuate the healing ward before the attackers arrived." He paused, his grin turning into a frown. "Now we owe you a debt of gratitude in addition to the debt of pain. We will never finish repaying everything we owe you."

He sounded genuine, and Prince Fenwick was a soldier, not a spymaster with superb acting skills. Clament wanted to believe him.

"They were coming after me. If I hadn't been there, the healers would never have been in danger."

Fenwick snorted. "You're only in the healers' ward at all thanks to Toval's incompetence. If we had trained and monitored the soldiers and healers in charge of the prisons properly, you would have still been behind a locked and guarded door where they never would have had a chance to target you in the first place."

More people jogged into view—soldiers, the other two healers, two more apprentice healers, more soldiers, and the obnoxiously curious who had no logical purpose for being there. Fenwick casually stepped closer to Clament as if he was moving out of the way of the path of those arriving, but he stood in a way that made it difficult for anyone to see Clament's face.

"The attackers had an informant," Clament said before his reason returned. Clament firmly believed the attackers had been sent from Namin, which meant either his father or older brother had authorized it. He should have expected this to happen when Toval didn't simply hang him and be done with it, but he still felt the cold burn of betrayal like a vise around his heart.

"They would have had to, in order to know you were in the healing ward rather than the dungeon," Fenwick replied, but his frown had turned into a scowl. "Did they say anything specific?"

"That Prince Braxton had left and this time of day the healing ward was emptiest so they would have the easiest time getting inside. Healer Alina and I were more interested in escaping at that point, so I didn't hear more."

"It's more than enough," Fenwick said, his voice an angry growl. "The list of people who know you're here in Toval is fairly small. The list of people who knew you were in the healing ward specifically is considerably smaller. And the list of people who knew Braxton was leaving is miniscule. What you told me should be enough to ferret out the informant."

Alina emerged from the crowd, pushing a wheeled chair in front of her. Clament's patchwork blanket was folded neatly on the seat. A second chair followed her, but the two healers with that chair went over to gather Loweseth. Alina unfolded the blanket and draped it over Clament's shoulders, tucking the edges high so it partially obscured his face.

"He can't stay in the ward tonight," Alina told Fenwick as she supported Clament in standing on shaking, exhausted legs, then transferring over to the wheeled chair. "We're going to be weeks repairing everything."

Fenwick's mischievous grin returned. "I know just the place.

Guarded, yet very comfortable. Do you have a few minutes to spare to come inspect the location with us, healer?"

Alina nodded. "Lead the way." She took a few extra seconds to fuss over making sure Clament was comfortable, pulling the blanket even higher around his face in the process, before gripping the chair handles and pushing him along the hall after Fenwick. They stuck to less-used hallways, ones without windows so the only light was from evenly spaced lamps. Most of the people they passed wore some sort of servant or secretary uniform, and when they saw Fenwick they bowed low and hurried away without sparing much of a glance at Clament. When they reached a long hallway with widely spaced doors, Fenwick slowed so he was walking next to Alina.

"Were you able to take a look at the bodies?" he asked her.

"A quick one. Just enough to check what poison they used to be sure it wouldn't spread through the air. I didn't recognize them, but they each had an odd tattoo behind their right ears. A red star of some kind, but it didn't look right."

"Three interconnected triangles, each triangle a different shade of red?" Clament choked out, his voice strangled by the knot in his throat.

"Yes, exactly like that," Alina replied.

"You know what that star means," Fenwick said to Clament, his tone curious, but when Clament glanced up, Fenwick's eyes were sharp and serious.

Clament swallowed hard and then again when the first time didn't clear his throat enough to speak.

"Tell Braxton I'm ready to talk. About everything."

Interlude

THIS HIGH IN the Spikehorn Mountains, winter came early. Most of the trees and shrubs had lost their leaves, a scant few resplendent in reds and oranges clinging to the otherwise bare branches. Braxton was a little surprised he hadn't encountered any measurable snow on the journey here. Back in Etoval, the trees were a full a riot of color, despite the occasional flurry. He crouched in the brush, letting those remaining leaves help conceal him, and squinted through his binoculars at the campfire merrily burning in a small clearing caused by a fallen tree. A man huddled there, his hands out to the fire. Braxton glanced at his watch briefly before returning his attention to the man. Another thirty seconds went by before the man reached into the pack next to him, pulled something out, and threw it on the fire.

The flames flared, glowing a strange blue green for a brief moment, before subsiding to normal orange red.

"That's the signal," Braxton whispered. An answering rustle from the two people who had traveled with him on this mission was his only re-sponse. He extricated himself from beneath the bush, tucked the binoculars away, and headed down the hill. Shir stayed close, guarding Braxton's back, while Davon stayed behind, hidden in case of an ambush.

The man by the fire looked up as Braxton approached but didn't stand. Braxton only knew him by the name Ama. His hair and eyes were ordinary shades of brown—although the hair might be dyed and the eyes magicked. His skin was lightly tanned, a color that could be seen in most kingdoms but could also be the result of rubbing juiced nutberry on the exposed areas, which temporarily darkened the skin for a few days. Ama claimed he was eighteen years old, but he had been claiming that for the five years Braxton had known him. He didn't look older than midtwenties, but again, that could be a ruse. All Braxton could really confirm about Ama was he was incredibly trustworthy as a spy for Toval. Braxton couldn't say why Ama had chosen Toval to support, but Braxton had never once doubted the intelligence Ama provided.

Most of the time Ama traveled to Braxton to report or sent infor-mation in coded letters. On rare occasions, Ama couldn't afford the time it took to travel all the way to Toval, when he had information that needed to be delivered in person, so Braxton met him halfway. Most people traveled through the Spikehorn Mountains with caution and in large groups. Ama traveled alone and never seemed bothered by the danger.

"The great all-knowing king is furious." Ama's voice was gentle but also unremarkable. If Braxton heard Ama speaking in a crowd, he wouldn't be able to pinpoint the speaker.

"The king of Namin is always furious. What's caught his attention this time?"

"You didn't kill his son, of course," Ama replied with an easy shrug. "The unwanted. The bastard. Sent to Toval as a distraction, but also in the hopes he would die at the hands of a Tovalian prince so Namin could have an excuse to declare war."

Braxton frowned, trying to parse through everything Ama was saying. "That damned king has been mad at us before. That's nothing new, although it would explain the information I've been receiving about Namin forces amassing in the south."

Ama shook his head. "You're not listening, princeling. The unwanted son is who angered the all-knowing for daring to survive and thereby thwart their plans. The all-knowing now believes the bastard son dying while under Toval's protections would serve the same purpose so has sent people to ensure that occurs."

Braxton didn't know why Ama kept calling the Namin prince "unwanted" or "bastard"—probably for the same reason he referred to King Cyphus as "all-knowing" rather than by name—but there was only one Namin prince currently living in Toval.

"Clament!" Braxton gasped, surging to his feet, his heart thudding in his throat. He had to get back to increase protection around Clament. Braxton wouldn't—couldn't—allow anything to happen to stubborn, beautiful, far-too-enticing Clament, especially not after everything Clament had already suffered due to Braxton's incompetence.

Ama rested the tips of his fingers against Braxton's forearm. "Whatever they planned has already happened. Even if you rush home now, you will not reach him in time. It's much more important to stay and hear the rest of my information."

Braxton clenched his fists and growled. His heart hadn't slowed, and all he wanted, with every fiber of his being, was to know Clament was okay. Braxton just plain liked him. Clament was sweet and stubborn, sad and desperate for attention, and Braxton wanted to be the one to bring a smile to his face. What had started as a simple task to obtain information from an enemy prince had evolved to so much more in the past few months, particularly in the last couple weeks while Clament had been recuperating and they had been able to actually have conversations.

"Why do you call him unwanted?" Braxton asked, trying to distract himself. He crouched back down next to the fire.

Ama shrugged. "It's the same as his actual name. But that's not my tale to tell. You will have to ask him. Instead, you should be asking me what else the all-knowing has directed his fury toward."

"Okay, I'll bite. What else?"

"The harvest failed in Namin. Not through drought, but through gross mismanagement. The king demanded his tithe. The lords demanded theirs. And once the tithes were stolen, the farmers did not have enough seed remaining to plant this past spring. No one has gotten their tithes this autumn, and starvation is the least of Namin's worries this winter. The all-knowing has seen coup plotters around every corner, and you have heard of his forces testing Toval's southern border. He doesn't want those farms. He *needs* them. Coup plotters can't keep falling off parapets or drowning in moats before suspicions arise, and those who ascribe to the all-knowing's enemies grow to levels he can't suppress.

"To solve everything, he is building a military fortress in these mountains. He will have the height advantage, and will be able to position troops and supplies closer to Toval for when he is ready to plunder. He is also using it as a base to recruit spies in the name of Randolph to keep Toval focused on defeating that enemy rather than focusing exclusively on Namin."

Braxton pinched the bridge of his nose, trying to stave off an oncoming headache and understanding now why Ama couldn't put this intelligence in writing.

"Do you know where?"

Ama shook his head. "I'm sorry. Not yet. The reason I wanted to meet here is so I can go deeper into the mountains to try to find it and get you more information."

"Anything you can get on the location, on any weaknesses, or anything we can use to dismantle that fortress before Namin attacks with more than spies and evil stories, and I'll double your earnings." Braxton let out a heavy sigh, ran a hand through his hair, and pretended he didn't see the gleam in Ama's eyes at the mention of money. Ama's decision to work for Toval might be a mystery, but why he continued to provide such excellent information wasn't. He needed money badly, but given the value of everything Ama had just provided, Braxton had zero issue with providing as much as Ama wanted. Of course, that could be yet another ruse to keep Braxton complacent by believing he had figured out Ama's motivation. Since Ama had yet to provide bad intelligence, Braxton didn't honestly care. All he cared about was stopping Namin before they amassed their army and started killing Tovalians and to get back home as quickly as possible so he could halt the churning in his gut when he learned whether Clament was still alive.

"I'll be in touch as soon as I learn more." Ama stood and quickly upended a water skin over the fire, dousing the flames and sending smoke up in a plume.

"Stay safe," Braxton responded, coughing and waving the smoke out of his face. When the smoke cleared, Ama was gone. Braxton ought to be used to Ama by now, but he still got a tightness in between his shoulder blades—as if a target were painted there—every time Ama did one of his disappearing acts.

Braxton took a second to ensure the fire was actually out before waving to Shir and Davon.

"Back to the castle as fast as we can go," he explained, already leading the way out of the clearing to where they had left the horses about a half mile away. The entire journey to the horses, and then the entire two-day trip back to Etoval, Braxton worried: Worry about Namin and that damned fortress they were building somewhere in the densely wooded, extremely dangerous Spikehorn Mountains. Worry about whether Clament was still alive, and if he was, whether he had been hurt again. And worry for himself, because as long as these crazy, churning feelings that erupted every time he thought about Clament continued, Braxton knew his life as a happily single bachelor was probably over.

Chapter Five

GENTLE FLURRIES OF snow blew outside Clament's window, the first signs of the coming winter as the chill of late autumn truly settled across the land. The fat white flakes drifted downward, where they immediately melted on the flagstones far, far below. The season was far too young for any snow to accumulate just yet. The royal wing of the palace comprised the top two floors and tower on the western section of the castle, and Clament had been given one of the smaller, one-story rooms. He let the curtain fall and turned around to survey his space for the thousandth time, still in disbelief that Fenwick had allowed him access to so much luxury.

The chair Clament was sitting in was part of a small breakfast nook tucked under the window, out of which he had just been looking. Gleaming, golden wood floors spanned the space covered with thick area rugs of geometric shapes in dark gray and green. Two cream-colored couches with green scatter cushions surrounded an oval coffee table stained dark brown.

By the door, a matching entry table with places for correspondence, keys, and other miscellany, and a matching sideboard, with crystal cut decanters full of brandy and gin, spanned the back wall. To the left was the door to the office, which had another green and gray rug and a desk in that same dark wood that dominated the room. Clament had no use for an office, so it was empty aside from a bookcase near the door, where he kept some of the books the castle library had loaned him.

The bedroom was equally well-appointed, a massive four-poster bed with green curtains and a dark gray blanket over a mattress so sinfully soft most mornings Clament had to convince himself to get out of bed. Dark-stained nightstands framed either side of the bed, and a dressing table with a mirror filled the wall opposite the windows. Another door led to a closet the same size as the office, the shelves almost completely empty aside from his handful of borrowed outfits. Through the closet was an actual bathing room with running water. A tub and shower, a flush toilet, and a sink in beautiful, gray-threaded marble. Clament had heard of the new magic and technology that allowed for running water, but had never seen it used for such luxury. The castle where he grew up in Namin certainly couldn't boast such extravagance.

A gentle knock sounded on the door. Clament looked away from the snow toward the sound and called out, "Enter."

The door opened and the usual servant who tended Clament's room stepped inside. "Prince Braxton asked if he might come by to speak with you, Your Highness."

Finally. Clament controlled his face so he didn't show his worry, but the churning in his stomach and his heart rate increased.

"Whenever he's available, please tell him he's welcome," Clament responded, glad his voice didn't crack or sound strangled.

The servant bowed and left, closing the door behind him. Clament wanted to get up and pace; his legs ached to move to relieve some of the tension, but his legs also still ached because of the abuse he had inflicted on them six days ago, running from his attackers. Also, Alina would subject him to more of her nasty concoctions if she found out he was moving around too much. Clament compromised by only moving over to one of the couches where his patchwork quilt was neatly folded.

Another minute passed and Clament started to worry Braxton wouldn't have time to come by until later, but then another knock sounded, this one firmer and louder than the previous.

"Come in!"

Braxton walked inside, closed the door behind him, and then awkwardly stood in the entryway staring at Clament. Clament wanted to believe he saw genuine relief in Braxton's lovely hazel eyes as he looked at Clament for a long moment.

Clament wanted to be able to tell Braxton everything, exactly like he had said to Fenwick. But while his statement to Fenwick was about who had tried to kill him and why, right now the small, secret part of Clament really wanted to explore the way his insides were melting and squirming under Braxton's regard. Beautiful eyes, set in a face that Clament had only allowed himself to dream about when he was alone, looked at him as if he mattered—Clament, the useless, throwaway prince of a country that didn't want him. That seemed too far-fetched, though, and distracting himself by looking at those beautiful eyes and dreaming about such nonsense wasn't helpful. Clament needed to focus on reality, not speculation. He firmly shoved away his errant thoughts, turning his attention back to the fact that

Braxton had safely returned from his trip.

Thankfully, aside from looking tired, Braxton didn't appear to have suffered on his journey. His hair was still damp from a recent shower, the strands curling over his forehead and around his ears in a way Clament struggled not to call cute. Add a few droplets of water sliding down Braxton's suntanned skin, and Braxton would easily slide from cute to sexy. With a flash of panic that finally quelled the overexcited beating of his heart, Clament clamped down on that thought too. He shouldn't be thinking like this about an enemy prince. It was past time for Clament to get himself under control. Thankfully, Braxton spoke again, giving Clament a needed distraction.

"Alina said you were unharmed, and I'm glad to see she told the truth," Braxton said.

Clament belatedly waved to the opposite couch, realizing Braxton was waiting for an invitation to come closer. He ignored the stab of—he wouldn't call it jealousy —but some sort of dark, unpleasant jolt went through him, hearing Braxton had gone to speak with Alina first.

"I heard you had been attacked and had a moment of panic when I reached your room in the healers' ward and you weren't there. Alina told me Fen had you moved somewhere safer. I…um… When you were well enough to leave the ward, I was planning on moving you here anyway, so don't think you're taking someone's room or something. This was already prepared for you beforehand."

Clament hadn't considered that he might have displaced someone from their home, but it was nice to know all the same, particularly with the addition of the blooming warmth that filled him at the thought of Braxton thinking of him and planning ahead for his comfort. His earlier feelings…

Well, he still refused to call what he felt then jealousy, but at some point he was going to have to sit down and figure out what to do about his growing, swirling emotions when it came to Braxton. He had to get rid of them…or embrace them. The latter was impossible, so he had to do the former even though he was clearly failing miserably.

Either way, that warmth comforted him more than he wanted to admit.

"The room is wonderful," Clament replied and then shut his mouth hard when that came out a touch too wishful. He had resolved to tell Braxton about Namin's scheme; Braxton didn't need to know about how difficult life had been for Clament in Namin though. Letting Braxton know this was the nicest room he had ever lived in would only distract them from the real reason Braxton was here.

They lapsed into awkward silence for a few long moments before Braxton let out a heavy sigh.

"Right. Namin is building a fortress in the Spikehorn Mountains, somewhere south along the border with Toval," Braxton said, his tone stern, but his eyes soft and worried. "Their intent is to have better access to the border, troops stationed closer, supply lines closer, everything an invading army needs. And what Namin needs is food."

Clament let out his own sigh, dug deep to firm his resolve, clenched his fists, and jumped off the cliff's edge Braxton had dragged him to. "Not just food," Clament replied. "The military has been promised a grand victory over Toval for generations. Instead, the generals are plump and spoiled off the king's bribes, and the regular enlisted are starving, the same as the peasants. More sergeants and lieutenants have had mysterious accidents than the generals can conceal, and soon the coup will come from those trained to fight. There are still some lords who haven't fallen into the klep-tocracy, and they'll side with the military. Plus, the peasants will rise up and provide the numbers the coup needs to succeed. However, for all of that to occur, the military has to slip their chains first. The king knows all of that. Rather than allowing the military to plot in the capital, he sent them to the mountains where they would be distracted by building a ridiculous fortress Namin can't afford to build, all so they can have their promised victory over Toval rather than a coup against the Namin throne."

Clament ran his hands through his hair as he mentally reminded him-self why he had finally chosen to break his ties with Namin. Three red tri-angles, tattooed discretely on the people sent to kill him. He had been be-trayed first, in the worst way. He opened his mouth and the rest fell out in a rush of words, too fast to stop or temporize.

"The north was a distraction. The mercenaries were meant to pull your attention and your forces there, so Namin could begin making forays into the south. Small victories and some food plundered before winter would tide the military over until the spring when the fortress would be completed, and Namin could invade at full force while Toval was still dis-tracted rebuilding the north. I…erm…I did tell them the distraction plan would fail, but I suspect that my being killed by Toval was their contingency plan."

Braxton shook his head in disgust, and he didn't seem surprised by anything Clament was telling him. Well, he already knew about the secret fortress, so perhaps he had also known or guessed why Clament was leading that ridiculous band of mercenaries in a plot doomed to failure.

"Thank you for telling me," Braxton finally said, and his smile was small and gentle, with absolutely no sign of pity or disgust. "If you don't mind my asking, what made you change your mind? You were adamant before about not breaking your silence, to the point…" he trailed off, grimacing, but Clament could interpret. To the point that two guards and a so-called healer had taken it upon themselves to torture him to try convincing him to talk, but saying that out loud would be crass.

Rather than dwelling on what had gotten him to the healing ward in the first place, not daring to open the box where those memories were so carefully tucked away, Clament instead chose to focus on the event that had gotten him sent to the royal wing. He pulled over a small folder he had been doodling in the last time he had sat on the couch and flipped it open to reveal the top piece of paper covered in triangles.

"Terrorize, torture, and terminate. The three foundational principles of the Triumviré, an ancient term that roughly translates to three leaders. Children are chosen at birth to join them and trained from infancy in how to kill. Their only loyalty is to the king of Namin, who uses them as a threat against anyone who might think about unseating him. All the people who die mysteriously—heart attacks in their sleep, falling off a parapet in the night—the Triumviré are the culprits. By sending them to kill me, the king of Namin declared he sees me not just a traitor to Namin, but as a threat to his continued existence."

"Does he care at all that you're his son?" Braxton asked, his tone gentle as if he wasn't certain he ought to be asking that question. He was right, but the wound that question prodded was an old and long-scabbed-over one.

"Did whoever told you about the fortress also tell you about my name?" Clament didn't want to bring up the source of all his pain, or to explain his sordid past, but Braxton needed to understand the level of cruelty the king of Namin was capable of before he went up against him.

"They mentioned your name was an explanation but told me it was your story to tell and didn't elaborate." Braxton's eyes were soft as he looked at Clament, as if he was actually concerned he might be causing pain by bringing up the topic, and Clament had to look away before sorrow turned into pity.

"The king raped my mother, a servant whose job was to tend fires in the royal apartment. These days he's more careful, but back then he didn't bother with contraception. When I was born, my mother walked into the court at full session and declared what he had done to her, and I was the proof. He was forced to adopt me, and he named me Clament, with an A rather than the usual spelling with an E, because he couldn't name me La-ment outright. As the unwanted, bastard child, I am expendable—a tool to be used until I die, and even then, he planned to use my death as a rallying cry. Apparently, he decided to ensure I died here in Toval."

"If you don't mind my asking, how did the court prove you were the king's son? A newborn babe would hardly have any distinguishable fea-tures."

Clament laughed, but it wasn't a happy sound. "The royal power of Toval allows you to summon weapons from thin air. The royal power of Namin allows us to see danger before it arrives. They say the original kings and queens could see the past, present, and future, but these days we only see the present with premonitions when danger comes nearby."

"That's how you knew the attackers were on the way in the healing ward," Braxton said, nodding to himself as if that explained a lot.

"Yeah. I felt it when they made the decision to attack. The power couldn't activate when I was with the mercenaries because while every single one of them would have been very happy to take my head, none of them had decided to actually do it. I didn't realize how bad the situation had gotten until Prince Fenwick walked into the tent. Anyway, as children, the royal power leaks out until we learn to control it. Even as an infant, there was no concealing I had the power of kings."

Clament let out a breath and released his magic, a golden glow suffusing his vision. His third eye opened, but he didn't push the magic outward. He let Braxton see for a few moments, the way his pupils vanished beneath the golden sheen and the gold eye that opened between his brows, before clamping back down on the power to shut it off again. His vision returned to normal, and he looked over at Braxton, who simply smiled cheekily.

"I bet not all your siblings have that power, or if they do, it's not as strong."

That surprised a laugh out of Clament. "Yes. Only Cadell has the same amount of power as me, which is why he's the heir. If he could have, he would have sent the Triumviré after me years ago since I'm the biggest threat to his succession." Clament didn't bother telling Braxton about the years of torment that comprised his childhood, but he had a feeling Braxton guessed. "I didn't want to prove them right," Clament admitted. "That's why I didn't want to tell you anything. Until my father decided I was worth more to him dead than alive, that is."

Braxton shook his head. "Every time I hear something about your family I think surely they can't do anything worse. And then I learn something new and am disgusted all over again. They never bothered to get to know you—the real you. Did they?" He sighed and they lapsed into silence. Clament closed the folder, hiding away those damned triangles again and leaned deep into the couch cushions, resting his head against his quilt.

"If your family doesn't want you anymore," Braxton began, hesitant as if he wasn't certain he ought to be saying anything. "You could renounce them yourself."

Clament's mouth dropped open, and he stared at Braxton. "How would I do that?" he asked, except now that the thought was in his head, churning and bubbling and welcoming in a way not much else in his life had ever been, a sort of lightness came over him. He could renounce his father, who saw him only as a pawn, and his brother, who saw him only as someone to torment. He could toss off the false trappings of a prince and become someone completely new.

"Change your name to something that makes you happy rather than something that gives them evil feelings of glee. Your name should be one you can be proud of, reflects how good a person you are, and is used by people who care about you." Braxton shrugged. "That's where I'd start, but it's entirely your decision." He smiled and stood. "I'll leave you to think it over."

Braxton left, shutting the door gently behind him as if he knew those simple words had eased away all the complexities of what Clament had always seen as such a thorny issue. Clament curled up on the couch, pulled his quilt over him, and thought about those words for a long time, until Alina came by with his afternoon meds.

Chapter Six

PRINCE FENWICK DIDN'T live in the castle, Clament had learned. He lived in the military barracks some ways from the city, and apparently lived happily with the chef who had aided in Clament's capture. He kept a room in the royal wing, though, for when he needed to stay over for whatever reason. Fen, as he had asked to be called after their second lunch together, had only been in the castle and near the smaller castle barracks by sheer coincidence when Clament had been attacked. Over the last few days, he had been here more often. Clament assumed it was in reaction or preparation for Toval's response to Namin's plans. He stopped by to chat or for a quick lunch whenever he could, and Clament was actually starting to like him. Fen had really only captured Clament out of necessity, and because Namin had made it so incredibly easy for him to do so. Clament couldn't hold it against him.

Sometimes Fen brought Crown Prince Ayer along too. Ayer seemed equally nice, if a touch more aloof. He had a pronounced limp, but his mind was the sharpest Clament had ever encountered. He would make a fine king, unlike Clament's brother Cadell, crown prince of Namin, who had inherited their father's bad temperament. After meeting all the princes of Toval, Clament suspected the riches Namin was truly envious of weren't the abundant fields, but rather the way the royal family worked together to support one another and the country they served. Because Toval didn't serve them in the way the entire country of Namin danced attendance on their king. No, Toval was the exact opposite, and it was beautiful. No wonder Clament's cold, grasping father was so eager to destroy Toval.

And then there was Braxton: calm, understanding, and with such a lovely smile. Braxton was handsome and kind, and far more generous than Clament had ever expected an enemy prince to be. In fact, Clament had stopped waiting for the moment he would be returned to the dungeon, finally understanding there was no artifice when it came to how Braxton treated others. That didn't mean Clament was about to let his burgeoning feelings loose for anyone to see. He was still technically a prisoner, albeit only barely, and certainly a well-treated one. He wasn't about to make assumptions and let anyone—Braxton especially—know about his infatuation. If Clament's feelings weren't reciprocated, he would only be placing a burden on Braxton's shoulders by forcing him to endure Clament's unwanted attentions.

Sometimes all three of them descended on Clament for lunch, like today where they were all squeezed around his breakfast nook on the extra chairs some servants had brought in.

Their inane chatter slowed as the servants finished putting out the food and departed, bringing Clament back to the present and the thorny issues they were trying to collectively solve: how to counter everything Namin was throwing at Toval.

Except, Fen's first question was directed at Clament specifically.

"Have you given any more thought to changing your name? You said Braxton had mentioned it."

Clament laughed and tipped his head back, looking at the white-painted ceiling. Once he was certain his laugh wouldn't devolve into hysteria or tears, he looked back down and replied. "It's all I can think about when I'm not wracking my head trying to figure out where in the mountains my father would think to build an entire fortress." The opportunity to change how he identified himself, to change the entire identity of the unwanted bastard prince thrust upon him at birth, was far, far too tempting.

"Can we help with anything?" Braxton asked with what appeared to be genuine concern. He lifted one hand as if he wanted to rest it on Clament's shoulder in comfort, but instead dropped it to his fork.

"I, well, I had one idea," Clament hedged, wondering whether his idea was even worth saying aloud. "My father named me Lament, but my mother chose to call me beloved. My middle name is Caro, which in the ancient language means someone loved." It was a crazy, radical change, one he wasn't certain he deserved. His mother might have named him Caro, but she had died when he was barely a year old. He didn't really know what it meant to be loved, so could he really claim such a name as his own?

"Caro is a beautiful name," Ayer said.

"Everyone deserves to be loved," Braxton abruptly cut in, his words sending a jolt of surprise through Clament. It was as if he were reading Clament's thoughts. "Sometimes it just takes longer to find the right people."

Braxton's eyes were blazing and intense as he stared at Clament, full of some sort of intent Clament wasn't certain he dared interpret. What if he was wrong, and that wasn't love glaring at him; what if Braxton was simply a passionate person when it came to these things, and Clament was inserting his own feelings where they didn't belong?

"If you want to be called Caro, we'll call you Caro," Braxton continued, his voice deep and gravelly with emotion. "If you want to become Caro, we'll help you figure out exactly who Caro is. The question is, what do *you* want?"

He wanted Braxton. With every fiber of his being, he wanted to belong to Braxton, and to have Braxton belong to him in turn. He wanted to feel Braxton's arms around him, clutching him tight. He wanted more than that too. But Braxton didn't deserve a broken partner. Braxton deserved to have someone strong and whole at his side, supporting him as a partner ought. Clament couldn't do that. However, perhaps, just perhaps, Caro might be able to become that sort of person.

Caro's voice was slow and halting, but for the first time, his body felt light as if the burden of generations had fallen from his shoulders. "I want to be Caro. Please, help me become Caro."

The room was silent for a long moment while Caro stared at his hands in his lap, clasped and white-knuckled from the strength of his grip. Then a hand appeared in his field of vision. Small knife scars, calluses, and fingers thick with muscle, yet so gentle as it rested on top of Caro's for a brief moment, before reaching for Caro's chin and gently tilting his head up. Braxton's hazel eyes were soft but still with the same intensity, and Caro got lost in them, staring, rapt, and with no desire to ever look away.

"Welcome to Toval, Caro," Braxton said. His hand didn't leave, remaining under Caro's chin in a caress that sent a shiver down Caro's spine.

"Thank you," Caro whispered, his throat tight with unshed tears and his breath hitching because while Braxton's eyes might be soft as he looked at Caro, they roared with emotion all the same as if his eyes were simply windows into his heart. Clament might not be willing to believe it, but Caro definitely did. Braxton was looking at him—at Caro—with want and love and with so many emotions that Caro wanted to burst out with his own return feelings.

Someone cleared their throat, and Caro jumped, finally breaking eye contact with Braxton. He had forgotten about the other two people in the room. Caro half expected to see looks of derision on their faces as he glanced sheepishly over, but they were only smiling. Although Fen's grin had a touch of mischief in it.

"You're going to have to introduce him to Mother now, you realize," Fen said to Braxton, his grin growing.

Braxton groaned. "Do I have to?" He glared at both his brothers. "You're not going to tell her, are you?"

Ayer laughed. "You say that as if she doesn't already know. No one is as shrewd or discerning as our mother," he added to Caro, including him in their conversation as the brothers always did as if he belonged with them.

The usual sickly sour feeling of being an interloper tried to well up, but Caro fought it back. If Ayer wanted to include him, it meant Caro was supposed to be there. These brothers weren't the type to be passive-aggressive or go behind his back. No, if they wanted him to do something or go somewhere, they would tell him outright.

"I really should meet Queen Trina and King Aurelius to thank them for allowing me to stay here despite the difficulties I've caused," Caro replied.

Fen and Ayer snickered and, confused, Caro looked from them to Braxton. Braxton's cheeks were pink even as he glared at his brothers, which only increased Caro's confusion.

"Our mother is an excellent queen," Fen explained when Caro looked back over at him and Ayer. "However, when it comes to her children, these days what interests her the most is finding us happiness. By her definition."

"Fennn," Braxton said in a half-whining and half-pointed warning.

"Yes, yes." Fen waved his hand between them. "Sorry, Caro. I'll let Braxton explain the rest. Let me just say Mother is very interested in meeting you. Has Alina cleared you to walk around without a healer's supervision yet?"

"She said she received permission to take me to the royal gardens this afternoon," Caro replied. "If I'm able to walk there and back without any issues, she said I should be able to go there any time I'd like to get some fresh air."

"Excellent. Then, if you get permission, you'll be able to join us for breakfast tomorrow morning. Eight o'clock in the private dining room at the end of the hall. The door to the garden is right next to the dining room." The grin he shot Braxton was cheeky, but his smile gentled when he looked back at Caro. "We'd love if you'd come."

"Then if Alina says it's okay, I'll be there."

"Would you please just eat your lunch and get out of here?" Braxton groaned out, rubbing one hand across his face. "You gossip worse than some of the old fogies at court."

Ayer and Fen both laughed, Fen reaching out to ruffle Braxton's hair.

"Where's the fun if we can't torment you a little in return for how you treated us?" Fen replied, although he and Ayer did settle down and actually start eating.

Caro was sad they had to leave about ten minutes later, but Crown Prince Ayer and Commander of the Royal Forces Fenwick very likely had important duties to return to. That they had found time to stop by for lunch was amazing enough. Braxton must have just as much work, but he stayed behind, sitting in his chair and waiting for the door to close before he turned to look at Caro.

"Don't let them, or me, pressure you into anything," Braxton said, his tone an unhappy growl as he glanced back over at the door his brothers had just gone through. "If you're not feeling up to breakfast tomorrow, don't feel obligated to go."

"I would appreciate the company, actually," Caro answered honestly. "But I don't want to impose if breakfast is private time for your family."

"It's not—" Braxton cut himself off, shaking his head and grimacing. He let out a slow breath and when he looked up at Caro again, his cheeks were faintly pink. "My parents had an arranged marriage. My mother brought lucrative trade deals from Yaroi, particularly a significant reduction in shipping taxes across the Eiroi Strait. She met my father for the first time at their wedding, and she hated every second of the spectacle of an arranged political marriage. She and my father have become very good friends, and they have learned to love each other, but it is not the love of lovers, merely a form of deepest respect. She promised herself that all her children would marry for love and has fought tooth and nail to ensure that happens. Ayer and Shairon's marriages benefited Toval because she is as crafty and wily as a queen can be, but that aspect of it came much later. Mother invited the sons and daughters of our neighboring rulers who didn't have royal magic—Namin excluded, of course—to the palace."

Magic was genetic, passed down from parent to child. If a parent didn't have magic, a child couldn't inherit it. The last thing royal families wanted was to reveal the secrets of their particular golden magic to a potential future enemy. Which meant royal children with magic were carefully hoarded, and only children without magic were sent away as part of political marriages. Queen Trina didn't have the royal magic from Yaroi so had been sent to marry King Aurelius; however, all four of her children must have inherited the royal magic of Toval from their father since they all remained here.

"Mother let them meet," Braxton continued, "and when they fell in love, she brokered deals to cement them as political marriages in addition to marriages for love. Fen and I were too young at the time, and as the two younger children less necessary to pair up for political advantage. I'm sure if Fen hadn't met his chef, Charmaine Oba-Musen, Mother would have attempted the same scheme again, but she's quite pleased having a Musen with ties to the royal family."

A Musen! That explained a lot, particularly if Charmaine was also an Oba-Musen. The Musen family were practically royalty themselves, their capabilities in the kitchen legendary. Those with the prefix Oba also had the ability to neutralize poison, or so Caro had heard, since no Musen had willingly come to work in the palace at the royal city of Svental, Namin's capital, in generations. Caro didn't doubt there were Musens working in Svental itself, but they must know the stories of the royal family and wanted to avoid getting beheaded because the soup was too hot or the ice cream too cold.

"Which leaves me as her only unmatched child," Braxton finished, grimacing again. He paused, and when he looked at Caro, his eyes were fierce, blazing like twin suns. "You were captured as the result of a war, tortured horribly, and are still recovering." Caro flinched, but Braxton continued, bullishly forcing the words out as if he didn't dare stop. "What little you've told me about your childhood sounds like a nightmare as well. And right now, you're taking your life into your own hands and writing your future. No one can or should tell you what to do; you're making your own choices based on your own strengths. You are going to become Caro, in truth, rather than just in name. And the last thing I want is to interfere with that, or for my mother to force you into something you're not ready for or you don't want."

"What—" Caro closed his mouth, swallowed, and tried again. "What do you think you or your mother are going to force me into?"

Braxton's cheeks went even redder, but his eyes didn't lose an inch of that blazing intensity. "From the first moment I saw you, I thought you were beautiful. You were stubborn and fiery, loyal, and so brave. I looked forward to every time I came to see you in the dungeon, and I admired how strong you were. I especially admire you now, knowing what you were going through and how you still refused to talk." He swallowed hard, and his gaze turned anguished. "I realized I admired you too much, and I reduced the number of times I went to see you. Rather than daily, I started coming every other day. And then only a couple times a week. I was so afraid of what I might accidentally say or do, but that only allowed you to get sicker and gave those damned guards more opportunity to hurt you.

"If my mother didn't notice how upset I was when you were rushed to the healing ward—when I carried you there in desperation someone might be able to save you—then she definitely noticed when I went straight there after learning you were attacked. Reporting what I found to the king about Namin's activities should have been forefront in my activities when I returned to Etoval, and yet I ran to find you instead. You are… I liked you as Clament. I know I'll like you even more as Caro. But I want you to have the chance to figure out who Caro is without me even inadvertently guiding you. And definitely without my mother interfering."

Finding words to respond was almost impossible, Caro's thoughts spinning and churning until he couldn't settle on what to say or ask first. And yet, over and over the same words came to the forefront. Braxton *liked* him, and the way Braxton said that one word had been filled with so much raw emotion, an aching want that spoke of much more than mere *like*.

"I hated you, at first," Caro responded, his throat dry, but his words still surprisingly clear. Braxton flinched, but Caro plowed on. "You reminded me of my older brother, always in a position of power and using that power to hurt others. Everything you said, your every gesture and facial expression, I interpreted through that lens. I *wanted* to believe you were just as evil because it was easier. And then everything you said, every gesture and expression you made proved you were the exact opposite. I've spent the last few weeks incredibly confused, to be honest. What I do know—" Caro paused, collecting his thoughts and taking a few calming breaths as what he was about to say was the most difficult part. "What I do know is Caro wouldn't exist without you. Without your support and encouragement, I never would have even dreamed about leaving Clament and everything Clament stood for behind. Embracing a new future for myself without you still being part of it would literally be impossible. So, please, please stay with me." He was begging, tears glistening in his eyes, but Braxton immediately took Caro's reaching hands and clasped them in his own warm palms, his strong fingers surrounding Caro's smaller ones in an embrace as welcoming as if he had taken Caro into his arms.

"If you want me with you, I will always be with you. If you need to fly alone, I'll let you fly and remain below to catch you if you need me to." Braxton's eyes were damp, although his cheeks were dry and his smile wobbled.

Caro's cheeks were dripping with tears, and he sniffled even as he smiled. "You be my rock to ground me whenever I fly too high, and I'll learn how to be yours, and I think we'll both be okay."

He didn't know who bent forward first, but the kiss was chaste and sweet, punctuating their promise with a wonderful finality. Braxton's lips were warm and soft, and Caro didn't need anything more than this right now. There would be time for more later as Caro became more comfortable with his new self, and Braxton understood that completely.

Braxton drew away, smiling at Caro, his eyes now dry. "I believe Alina is supposed to be here soon. And I'm sure my secretaries are desperate for me to return to work." He sighed. "I'll definitely see you for breakfast tomorrow, either with my family if Alina clears you, or I'll come here." He stood and started heading toward the door, then paused and darted back. Their second kiss was powerful and bruising, yet still sweet: lips pressed firmly, arms tightly wrapped, and bubbling joy flowing between them. And then Braxton was gone, with one last glance back at the door as he fled, likely before reason overwhelmed him as it was threating to do with Caro.

The door slid shut and Caro flopped back onto the couch, twining his arms through his patchwork blanket. A touch of his lips confirmed he was smiling, and reignited the tingling. Caro let out a happy sigh, and for the first time in his life, he relaxed, luxuriating in knowing someone else cared about him.

Chapter Seven

THE WALK TO the royal gardens wasn't a long one. Alina paced at Caro's side, letting him take his time walking down the lush carpet in the richly understated and tastefully decorated hallway. This palace was completely different to the royal wing his father and brother occupied. They had covered every inch of their royal apartments in gold and jewels to emphasize their wealth and power to themselves and to anyone who they felt might need a visual representation. The simple elegance here in Toval really emphasized the difference between being secure in one's power versus needing to flaunt it because of insecurity.

Thankfully, before Caro could dwell too long on more of his birth family's faults, they reached a glassed door at the end of the hall with a guard standing in front of it.

"Prince Caro, Healer Alina," the guard said with a short bow. He brandished a key and unlocked the door, pulling it open and holding it wide for them. "Please enjoy."

"Thank you," Caro replied, echoed by Alina.

Caro hadn't needed to tell anyone about his new name. Alina had known it, all the servants had addressed him correctly, and now even the guard knew him. Caro suspected all three princes had been busy ensuring he would feel comfortable, and Caro had no idea how to express to them how much it meant to him.

"You look like the walk so far hasn't taxed you," Alina said, eying him critically as they went down a long, narrow hallway and then stepped out into the sunlight.

"I feel okay, actually," Caro admitted, tilting his head back to let the heat of the afternoon sunlight bathe his face. The air was crisp with the promise of the coming winter, yet still warm enough in the sunlight that Caro was comfortable in only a light jacket. "My legs aren't tired and my lungs don't ache." He still felt unsteady inside, enough to know he wasn't completely healed, but this was the best he had felt since before joining the mercenary companies in the woods all those weeks and months ago.

"Then let's walk for a bit longer until we find a bench."

Alina let him lead the way down the path, which wound throughout the rooftop garden. Small dwarf trees were brilliant shades of red, yellow, and orange, flaunting what remained of their late autumn colors. No fallen leaves littered the ground, so the gardeners must come through regularly. Bare branches were taking over from those covered in leaves, but the glory of the mix of bright colors was still evident. The last vestiges of late summer and fall flowers were in bloom, the mums vibrant and as multicolored as the trees. Dahlias and other flowers Caro couldn't name dotted the mulched beds. A narrow stream meandered through the garden, culminating in a small pond in the center. They stopped at the bench there where they could watch small, multicolored fish darting around.

"I thought the public gardens where the nobles and such gather were nice, but this is glorious," Alina breathed out, her voice awed and happy.

"I do think it's quite pretty," another voice called, her tone bright with laughter.

Caro and Alina spun around to see a woman walking toward them, two small children toddling down the path ahead of her, a nursemaid serenely trailing them.

"Don't get up!" she admonished when Alina started to jump to her feet. "I am here in an unofficial capacity. I snuck away from the office to take my children for an afternoon walk as a break from their lessons, so no need for any formalities. Besides, I'm tired of my brothers monopolizing you. I'm Shairon, second oldest after Ayer."

She looked like Braxton, with the same light brown hair and hazel eyes and general shape to her face, but she was willowy where he was stout, although Caro definitely believed she was just as strong.

"It's lovely to meet you, Prince Caro," she finished saying with another smile.

"It's lovely to meet you as well, Princess Shairon," Caro replied easily. She might have admonished him not to rise, but he did anyway, bowing over her hand as if they were both standing in court, all the nobles watching them jealously.

She laughed. "I hope you might be able to teach Brax some manners, although asking you to tame that buffoon is probably too big a task. Still, if you wanted to spend quite a long time trying, I don't believe Brax would mind." The knowing twinkle in her eyes had Caro's cheeks heating, but the earlier conversation he had with Braxton kept his chin held high.

"I wouldn't mind that either, my lady," Caro replied.

"None of that." Shairon wagged her finger at him, her eyes still twinkling happily. "Call me Shairon." Her expression turned stern, and she stood straight, suddenly looking regal and every inch a royal princess. "But if you hurt him or any of my family, the depths of pain I will subject you to will be far worse than anything you've ever experienced before. Understand?"

"I completely understand," Caro replied, liking her a lot and hoping his firm tone conveyed his equally firm conviction that he would never allow Braxton to get hurt when he was around to prevent it.

"Then I would like to add my welcome to my brothers' and welcome you to Etoval." Shairon's easy smile returned, but before she could say anything more, one of her kids ran up and tugged on her pants leg.

"Mummah, pretty fishies!"

He was maybe two years old and not exactly steady on his feet, but he dragged Shairon in the direction of the pond.

"I'll see you later," she called to Caro, before bending and grabbing up the tot, tickling him until he screeched with laughter. They reached the edge of the pond where the other one, who was maybe three years old, was lying on the edge, eyes rapt on the fish swimming below. The nursemaid was sitting at his side, but she moved out of the way when Shairon arrived.

"If you're ready, we should start heading back," Alina said. "Let them enjoy the pond."

"Right." Caro was already standing, but he waited for Alina to stand and dust off her green healer's robes before starting down the path back toward the door. They waved goodbye to the guard as they reached the hallway, but no one else was around as they walked to Caro's room. Once inside, Alina got Caro settled onto the couch, covered his legs with his quilt, and went to the tray she had left on the coffee table where a glass full of the familiar and hated glop was waiting.

"The princess scares me more than a drink full of healthy vitamins and minerals," Alina scolded when Caro grimaced and was slow to take the glass from her. "She's got so much more…" Her hands waved around her body to emphasize whatever nebulous presence to which Alina was referring. "If you're going to be spending time around her, you'll need all your strength, so drink up."

Caro sighed, but obeyed, forcing the bitter goop down as quickly as he could swallow, grateful when Alina passed him a glass of water next to help him clear away that awful taste.

Alina resettled the blankets over him again before sighing. "I have to get back to the ward, but send a servant to fetch me if you need anything. Okay?"

"Okay. Have a good rest of your afternoon!"

"You as well." She waved as she headed to the door, and then Caro was alone again.

He settled back into the couch cushions and pulled his quilt higher, snuggling into the comfortable fabric. An afternoon nap actually sounded pretty good at the moment, and maybe Caro would curl up with a book for a while after dinner.

And in the morning, he would meet the rest of Braxton's family.

He was sure they were nice people. Shairon had certainly seemed nice and aside from when Fen had captured Caro, he and Ayer both acted like decent people as well. Still, the idea of meeting the entire family in one swoop was daunting, and Caro really didn't want to dwell on the butterflies fluttering in his stomach that thought invoked. Instead, he closed his eyes and breathed slowly, trying to clear his head. He didn't know when he fell asleep, only that his naptime dreams were of flittering multicolored fish and Braxton's lips, pressing so wonderfully against his own.

Chapter Eight

CARO TOOK IN a deep breath and slowly let it out, attempting, and failing, to calm his nerves. On the other side of the closed door, in front of which he was awkwardly standing, was Braxton's entire family. Yes, Caro had met all of Braxton's siblings, but always in his own room—not in a formal setting like a dining room, and certainly not with the king and queen present. And, while he might be Caro now, a day of being a new person didn't magically erase the terrible things he had been part of as Clament.

A servant entered the hallway, heading toward Caro while holding a tray with a tureen and serving cups. Caro was in the way, so he wiped damp palms on his shirt, gripped the door handle, and pushed the door open.

He expected every eye to immediately turn in his direction, staring and accusing, but the only person who looked was Braxton, and he immediately smiled and jumped to his feet. He rushed over to Caro's side and took Caro's hand, guiding him to the empty place set next to Braxton's chair.

"You've met my brothers, Ayer and Fen," Braxton said, waving across the table to where Ayer sat next to a girl about six years old, sitting straight backed with her hands primly placed in her lap. Next to her was Fen, and next to Fen was another familiar face.

"Thank you for the chicken broth," Caro told Char, the chef who had aided in his capture and then selflessly helped him recover. "Alina—my healer—says she had to fight to keep everyone from stealing it. It was delicious."

Char smiled. "I'm glad you enjoyed it. You'll have to come visit my kitchen at the barracks some time so I can feed you some real food too."

"I'd like that. As soon as I'm cleared by the healers to walk farther than one hallway, I'll come by." Caro smiled, and Char returned the smile.

"This is my sister, Shairon," Braxton continued, sitting back so Caro could see her sitting on Braxton's other side.

"We've met," Shairon said dryly, winking at Caro and giving Braxton an impish grin.

"Oh, no," Braxton said, his tone only half joking.

"In the garden yesterday," Caro explained.

"Yes, we had a lovely chat," Shairon cut in. She leaned back to let the servant place a small bowl of what looked like cooked fruit to Caro's very untrained eye in front of her. When she leaned forward again, she was mock scowling at her brothers. "Why did I have to corner him in the garden to meet him? I should have been introduced ages ago."

The servant returned, placing bowls in front of Braxton first and then Caro. Hungry, Caro reached for his spoon, only remembering as his fingers touched the cool metal that he ought to wait for the king and queen to eat first and neither of them had started yet. Except a whoosh of magic ran through him, tingling from where his fingers touched the spoon up to his third eye. Danger had just entered his passive magical awareness.

"Don't eat!" Caro gasped out, his mouth moving even before his brain could connect the dots. He moved his hand from the spoon to the bowl of fruit thing and suddenly his vision gained a gold sheen. "Something's wrong with the food."

A crunch noise sounded, followed by a thud. Braxton jumped to his feet, followed by Fen, both of their chairs hitting the ground with twin bangs. Caro slowly turned to look, his heart beating in his throat. The body of the servant who had brought the fruit to the room twitched where it had fallen before lying still, white foam flecking the sides of his mouth. Braxton appeared completely calm as if he encountered things like this every day, and then he tilted the head to the side to look behind the ear.

"Not one of those Tri-people," he said with a shake of his head. "Just another regular spy."

Caro let out a breath he hadn't realized he had been holding and pressed his hands flat against the table to still their shaking. This attack on the royal family wasn't his fault. At least, not entirely.

"Did you eat anything?" Shairon asked her son, who was sitting in a special chair on her far side.

"No, Mummah."

Shairon let out her own relieved breath before turning to the rest of the table. "How did they sneak poison into our food? Don't we pay that Musen chef an exorbitant amount of money to prevent this?"

Char had been stirring his bowl, frowning as he carefully mixed the cooked fruit in sauce. He scooped up a small amount on his spoon and licked the edge where the juices were threatening to drip.

"Mushrooms. Who would think adding mushrooms to a bowl of fruit is a good idea?" Char exclaimed, sounding mortally offended, but when he looked up at Fen, his eyes were serious. "It's the same fool's mushrooms Roe used when she tried to kill us. Presuming we didn't notice something as ridiculously obvious as mushrooms mixed in fruit compote, we would have noticed when we all collapsed and died in a few hours, too late for a healer to save us. Because of the elapsed time, we would never be able to pinpoint exactly where the poison had come from. But," he added, looking at Shairon and then over to the king, who was frowning, the line between his eyebrows a deep crevasse. "I don't believe this compote came from my cousin's kitchen. Look at the consistency. They tried to use cornstarch to thicken this, rather than cooking it properly, which tells me it was made quickly and in secret. Besides, I've eaten breakfast in here with you enough times to know it usually comes with cloches and tea and multiple servants. I suspect our actual meal is still on its way, with Terrance's minimalist efforts fully engaged as usual."

"I believe Char has a point," King Aurelius said, still frowning. His eyes had appeared to be a lovely green blue, rather than the hazel of the queen and all their children, when Caro entered the room, but they were shaded to a deeper green by his lowered brows as his frown grew. "I am also wondering what their larger plan was. Killing the entirety of the royal family would have destabilized Toval, but not irrevocably. My cousin, Pauline, Duke Lefoile, would have become queen, and she would have very successfully kept Toval together while enacting revenge for our deaths."

"So either this was a crime of opportunity, where this servant saw his chance and took it, or there's a larger plan at work." Queen Trina finished.

"Exactly," Aurelius said with a nod. "Fen, find some people you know you can trust to remove this body and safely dispose of this concoction in complete secrecy. Braxton, summon a servant to retrieve Healer Alina to come see Prince Caro. She comes to this wing regularly, so her presence wouldn't seem odd, and we can ensure none of us have been poisoned this morning without giving away that we know about this plot."

He paused and looked slowly around the room, catching everyone's eyes in turn with his own. When he reached Caro, Caro was grabbed by the intensity King Aurelius exuded, as if there were magnets hidden in the pupils of his green eyes. Charismatic, a drawing pull that he had definitely passed down to Braxton since Caro felt the same thing when Braxton looked at him with similar levels of intensity. And yet, there was nothing accusatory about it, nothing angry or suspicious. He was simply including Caro with the rest of his family, gauging his willingness to participate and welcoming him into their plan to combat this plot.

"Char, you are certain this is a slower-acting poison?" When Char nodded, Aurelius continued. "Healer Alina will tell us when this poison would have killed us. I suggest we all disappear from public view at about that time and see what, if anything, might crawl out of the woodwork. And we should be prepared to squish whatever that might be," he added, a slow grin brightening his face.

The grin was echoed by all four of Aurelius's children and his wife. Fen and Braxton left the room, and Char followed, saying something about delaying the kitchens for long enough as he went. Caro huddled in his chair, wishing there was something more he could do to help stop Namin from constantly targeting this wonderful family.

Shairon stood and walked over to him, bending and wrapping her arms around him. "Thank you," she whispered into his ear. "Thank you so much for saving my family."

"It wasn't me. It was my magic. It's automatic when I'm threatened." Caro shrugged, but he reached up and gripped her wrists where her hands rested across his chest.

"You could have stayed quiet, but instead you chose to save us. Thank you, Caro. Thank you so much."

Interlude

BRAXTON FOLLOWED FEN into the hallway, but while Fen vanished through a secret door behind a convenient painting, heading through the secret passages to obtain the help he needed, Braxton went to Caro's room. Once inside, he quickly closed the door between the bedroom and sitting room, lowered the shades in the sitting room to imply Caro hadn't yet left the bedroom, and then yanked on the bellpull to summon a servant.

"Prince Caro isn't feeling well this morning," Braxton lied when the servant arrived. "Please have Healer Alina summoned, but quietly," he admonished. "No need to worry anyone else."

"At once, Your Highness." The servant bowed and hurried off.

Braxton collapsed onto the couch to wait, sighing as he tipped his head back against the cushions and trailed his fingers along the beautiful quilt Caro had clearly fallen in love with.

What a day, and all before breakfast.

As horrible as it sounded, Braxton knew he focused more on the uniform than on the face when it came to the servants who worked in the castle. There were hundreds of them, and they were all paid well, with food, clothes, and housing also provided. But they were completely interchangeable. Braxton was always polite to the servants who kept the building running in ways even he didn't understand, and he certainly expressed his thanks for all their hard work. However, he couldn't provide a name or any additional information about the servant he had just sent to the healing ward, and that was unacceptable. Things would have to change if they were going to ensure a trusted and trustworthy cadre of servants continued to work in the royal wing. The pay and benefits might keep many of them happy, but being treated as little better than a warm body, completely exchangeable with any and every other servant in the building, did not engender much appreciation of those being served. Feelings of resentment would fester—highly exploitable by enemies like Namin. Fostering a different environment was going to take a lot of effort but was definitely worth it. Without Caro there today…Braxton shuddered.

They probably wouldn't have known they were poisoned. Well, actually, Char probably would have realized the second he tasted the dish, but since he hadn't cooked, stirred, or otherwise helped prepare it, his passive magic ability to neutralize poison wouldn't have kicked in. Maybe with Char's help they would have reached a healer in time. Maybe. But thanks to Caro, they didn't have to worry about it.

Braxton wasn't sure whether Caro's dismissal of their thanks was because he was shy—he was definitely far shyer than Clament, as Caro let himself be himself with the barriers down—or because he still didn't think anything he contributed had value. His low value of his own self-worth, to

Caro, meant the truth of everything he had accomplished didn't matter; he only saw the negatives. Braxton desperately wanted to sweep Caro into his arms and hold him tight, to thank him for existing. Except, Caro wouldn't understand Braxton. Not yet, at least, but Braxton was hoping as Caro threw off more of his terrible past and slowly became more certain of his future that would change too.

Alina flew into the room, not bothering to knock, and glanced around, her eyes wide and frantic.

"Where is he? Is he okay?" she forced out between panting breaths.

"Caro's fine. He's not sick. Sorry for scaring you," Braxton said quickly, holding out his hands in apology. "This was the most discrete way we could think of to get a healer to the royal wing without arousing suspicion."

Alina frowned and straightened as she caught her breath. "What happened?"

"Someone tried to poison us all this morning. We believe they failed, but we're hoping you could look us over to double-check?"

"Poison! Of course I can check. Were you one of the targets? Come here!"

Braxton obeyed, submitting to her green-glowing hands as she used her magic to check him over.

"You're fine," she said after a long moment. "Take me to everyone else, please."

Braxton led the way out of Caro's room and down the hall to the dining room. Three people in the off-duty uniform of the royal guard—brown pants and a white shirt—were leaning over the poisoner's body when Braxton held the door open for Alina and then followed her inside. Braxton recognized Jensen, Fen's second in command, but didn't know the other two.

"Anything?" Braxton asked. Alina headed straight to the king and queen, her hands already glowing again.

"Nothing," Jensen responded with a sniff of disgust. "It's the same as when Roe tried to kill us. Dump poison into our food, then take a faster-acting version after discovery. I don't know about this servant, but Roe had been with us for six years without any sort of hint she was a traitor. We still don't know if she infiltrated to start or was turned later, and I doubt we'll learn anything more from this servant." He sighed. "Still, I'll let you know if we do learn anything else." Jensen waved at the other two soldiers, who started wrapping the body in cloth. Once they were done, the package definitely looked suspicious, but the body itself was concealed, and they left. Jensen hefted the tureen full of what was left of the fruit, all the filled dishes piled on top, then followed.

"Everyone is perfectly fine," Alina called as she stood from where she had been examining Shairon's kids and husband.

"Excellent. Thank you for checking," Father said. "Someone summon Charmaine and our real breakfasts, and then we should discuss how we're going to catch whoever comes to take advantage of our untimely deaths."

"Jensen will investigate the servant," Fen explained, walking to the door to no doubt pry Char out of the castle kitchens where, if Braxton knew Char, he had gotten distracted from his mission of delaying their breakfasts. He had likely ditched the less than stellar efforts of his chef cousin, Terrance, and was remaking their breakfasts from scratch. "I've summoned Zain to set up protection and to capture anyone who shows up.

She should be here by the time we've finished eating."

Braxton retook his seat next to Caro, gently resting his fingers over-top of where Caro's arm leaned against the table edge, then turned to look at Alina. "Please, stay for breakfast. And for afterward. I think it might be good to have a healer of your talents on board to help us fight this."

"Precisely," Father added. "For now, let's eat. Once Captain Zain arrives, we will go over the plan."

Chapter Nine

CARO SAT ON a sinfully soft couch in the king's solar, wishing he had his quilt to hide behind. Fen and the king were with some of Fen's troops hidden in some sort of space behind the throne room. Shairon was in the nursery, with her own sword, her scholarly husband, to whom Caro had barely been introduced at breakfast, and a cadre of troops. The children were napping in the queen's bedroom, down the hall from the solar. Braxton was off somewhere secretive, which aligned with his being Toval's spymaster, but Caro wished he was sitting next to Braxton on the couch. Instead, Caro was sitting across from Ayer and the queen, both of whom looked like they were only waiting for a quiet moment to start interrogating him. More of Fen's soldiers were in the room with them, and Caro was definitely getting side-eye looks from a couple who recognized him.

The clock chimed two in the afternoon, two quick bongs. "Healer Alina said the poison should have taken effect around now," Queen Trina called. "Brace yourselves."

Except, nothing happened. The last echo from inside the clock faded away, leaving them in silence with no sign anything might occur. Of course, them being attacked or the enemy coming to verify their deaths from the poisoning was only speculation. Seconds ticked into minutes, Caro sitting stiff with his fists clenched, listening along with everyone else for the slightest hint of an imminent attack. A scrape of metal as a sword left its sheath, a tap of booted feet on stone, or even a whisper of voices as last-minute commands were passed. Why Caro thought he would hear any of that from inside a secured room, he had no idea, but as five minutes became ten and then fifteen, he strained his ears for even the slightest hint. Perhaps no one was coming, and all their preparations were for naught.

Caro fidgeted, realized he was showing his nerves, and forced himself to stillness, only to find a moment later he was holding his breath. He ought to be used to things like this, the dread-inducing anticipation of a coming battle and then the battle itself. He had experienced similar situations many times before, but from the Namin side, being forced to participate in battles and events out of a nebulous sense of obligation to a family that always hoped the latest fight they sent him to would be his last. This time was different. This time Caro wanted to live, and he wanted the new family he was hoping he was making to be safe as well. The waiting, the wondering where the attack was going to come from—presuming there was even an attack on its way—was excruciating.

Caro closed his eyes and reached out with his magic. He didn't open his third eye, just let the power trickle free from its leash to sense anything nearby. He didn't feel anything though. Ayer and the queen were at peace with themselves and the situation. The guards were anticipatory but aware they might only be there as a precautionary measure. The nurses watching the children were ready, daggers hidden but easily accessible. Behind Caro more anticipation could be felt, similar to that of the guards—a readiness to strike when needed, but waiting for a signal for attack, and therefore not yet a threat.

Except no one was standing behind Caro's couch. Caro jumped up and spun to look at the line of bookcases stuffed full of books and tchotchkes.

"Caro?" Ayer asked.

"Is there a secret passage behind there?" Caro asked, keeping his voice low to prevent anyone waiting on the other side from overhearing.

"Not that I'm aware of," Queen Trina replied, standing as well. "But this is the oldest section of the castle, so I wouldn't be surprised if much of the original footprint has faded from living memory." She waved the soldiers forward, although they were already moving. About half remained near the door, the rest spreading in a semicircle around the bookcases.

"They all must be writhing in agony right now, poor poisoned bastards," Caro heard, although he was aware no one else in the solar could. "Let's move."

Caro's third eye flew open, glowing gold and pointing out the imminent threat as his passive magic field jumped to the fore.

"They're coming," he hissed, squinting through the sheen of gold across his vision as the bookcase on the right slid backward on silent hinges and then sideways to clear the opening.

The men and women who dashed out, swords and long knives drawn and fierce scowls on their face, were not expecting to run into the waiting soldiers. The man in the front yelled and swung, only to be batted aside by two soldiers. The attackers were hampered by the narrow opening, so they could only run out singly or in pairs, and Fen's forces handled them easily. They also were clearly not as well trained as Fen's Royal Forces—something Caro had learned firsthand not too long ago. The fight was over within minutes. Some of the attackers were dead, and some lay on the floor, moaning and bleeding. Others had surrendered, and still more were retreating down the passageway, the slap of their running footsteps and panicked yells echoing back up into the solar.

Fen's soldiers didn't need to pause to reorganize. A third of them immediately began pursuit, vanishing down the passage, a third stayed to triage the wounded and watch the captives, and the final third were still by the main door, guarding the other entrance.

Caro cast around with his magic, trying to sense anyone else hiding within the walls, but came up with nothing. He wished he had a sword or a blade of some kind—everyone else, including the limping Ayer had one— but Caro knew his limitations. It wasn't that they didn't trust him; the problem was he still wasn't strong enough. He could barely walk all the way down the hall; the exertion of swinging a sword was well beyond him. Besides, he wasn't exactly competent with a sword anyway. His lessons as a child had been minimal, just enough to serve as his brother's punching bag slash practice dummy. Even his magic lessons, the most comprehensive of his lessons, had only occurred to protect the secrets of the royal family. Once he was capable enough not to spill state secrets, those classes had stopped too.

All of which meant Caro stood in place and watched as everyone else around him did the hard work. He could only hope his small contribution of his magic-powered sight made up for the rest of his shortcomings.

"It would seem we are in your debt again," Queen Trina said, a soft smile tilting her rose-colored lips.

Caro swallowed hard, grabbed for his courage and the sweet memory of Braxton's lips against his, and replied, "Favors aren't owed between family."

Her smile grew. "No, they're not." She suddenly clapped her hands and called in a louder voice, "Right. Let's finish mopping up this mess. I want a report from the other groups, and then I want to get back to my day." People sprang into action, but Caro sank back down onto the couch cushions to rest his legs. He felt a little better every day, but jealousy still reared its head as he watched people dash off with their fully functioning bodies.

Queen Trina sat on the couch across from him, her eyes shrewd and far too knowing as she studied him—so much like Braxton's. "How long until Healer Alina thinks you'll be fully healed?"

Caro blinked, hoping his surprise that she appeared to be reading his thoughts didn't show on his face. "Another week or two, she thinks, before she'll allow me to return to regular activities," Caro replied. "We're working on strengthening my body, which she says isn't going to be an immediate fix."

Queen Trina was silent for a few long moments, apparently oblivious to the chaos around them as prisoners were carted off, the wounded were treated, and bodies dealt with.

"All of my children are warriors and they throw themselves into danger time and again to protect this country and the people they love," she began. Her face was somehow shadowed, as if the weight of what she was saying manifested visibly. "Fen and Shairon have their duties with the various military components they lead. Being surrounded at all times by other soldiers at least offers them some protection from attackers. Ayer is the crown prince so is constantly surrounded by guards, and because of his injury he cannot be on the front lines of a war. But Braxton is different. He slinks through the darkness, alone, with no one to watch his back." The shadows melted away, replaced by sheer intensity as her eyes blazed like twin flames as she froze Caro with her gaze. "Can you be that person for him? Can you look into the dark places and warn him of the danger, to be his eyes when the darkness tries to engulf him?"

Caro's heart was thudding so hard he thought she might be able to hear it, and his hands, where he had them clasped in his lap, were shaking. Still, it wasn't hard to find those intense feelings always simmering under the surface, waiting for the next moment he would find time to think about Braxton and how much he meant to Caro. His eyes were blazing when he replied.

"That's everything I want."

"Good," she said with a sharp nod before abruptly standing and turning to the half-dozen secretaries who had been hovering, waiting for their conversation to conclude.

Caro relaxed into the scattered couch cushions, knowing better than to escape from the overwhelming noise and bustle to the quiet of his own rooms, no matter how much he desperately craved some time to unpack his swirling, buzzing thoughts after that rather odd conversation. Instead, he did his best to stay out of the way.

Thankfully, Braxton swept into the room a few minutes later, his father and brother in his wake. Caro's greedy eyes took in Braxton's form, desperately searching for any sign of injury and thankfully finding nothing.

Braxton shot a quick smile in Caro's direction, but he headed over to his mother.

"I received word from one of my informants. He located the fortress in the mountains. Fen sent a team of forward scouts to obtain more information, but we should follow immediately."

"Let's not be hasty," Queen Trina replied after a glance at her husband. "Namin might already have their entire army stationed there, or they might only have unarmed civilian builders. We need to know more first before we can adequately plan. Plus, we need time to amass supplies and outfit soldiers. The scouts should be back in no more than two weeks, which is when we will make our final decisions and move out. Also," she looked between Braxton and Caro. "In two weeks, Caro will be fit to travel. I want him with you."

"Agreed," King Aurelius added when Fen and Braxton both opened their mouths to argue. "It is time we bring today back on track," he continued. "Let's all return to our regular duties and begin preparing to travel into the mountains to stop Namin once and for all."

Chapter Ten

THE LAST TIME Caro was in these mountains, the Spikehorn Range, he had been attempting to lead that doomed-to-failure diversion attack against Toval. Caro had known about the fortress being built in the south to support those attacks, but he didn't know exactly where or any other logistics. Fen's destroying the mercenary part of the plot hadn't been a relief to Caro at the time, but as he turned his horse to steady her, he caught a glimpse of Braxton glancing over at him, and he was glad, yet again, he had somehow survived against all the odds stacked against him.

Caro didn't know if he would ever be back to 100 percent health, but he certainly wasn't finding it too difficult to stay on a horse at the slow pace necessitated by the narrow path. Tall, old-growth trees towered overhead, their leaves a brilliant riot of reds, oranges, and yellows. This far south, autumn was still in full bloom. Back in Etoval, winter had started hooking her claws into the weather, with hints of the icy winds to come and the occasional snow flurry. They had a few weeks yet before the real snows started, or so Shairon had told Caro when she was helping outfit him for this trip. Namin had winter, but not like the depth of snow and ice Shairon described for Toval.

Craggy rock also bordered the path, which admittedly was little more than a game trail, so it wasn't possible to ride side by side. Instead, Braxton kept looking over his shoulder at Caro, as if needing to reassure himself Caro hadn't experienced a moment of weakness and fallen off his horse. And as if Alina wasn't on the horse behind Caro, also watching for that exact same thing.

On the one hand, of course, Caro appreciated their care and concern. On the other, knowing they didn't trust him to tell them when he needed a break was grating. The next time Braxton glanced around, Caro made a face at him, crossing his eyes and sticking out his tongue. Braxton grinned and returned to looking forward. He didn't look back again until the scouting team leading them called a halt a couple hours later.

They were in a small clearing, branches with colorful leaves arching overhead and more leaves turning brown underfoot. Caro dismounted and handed off his reins to the woman who trotted over to take them. He didn't have any duties to help make camp, so Caro joined Braxton and the rest of the command group off to the side of the clearing, where they were out of the way of the bustle.

Braxton was unrolling the rough map the scouting team had made when Caro reached him.

"Where are we on this?" he asked Captain Grall, a man in his forties who didn't look a day younger than sixty, his face a craggy, imposing mass of wrinkles, scars, and broken bones not realigned properly.

"Here," Grall replied, stabbing one finger at a spot dotted onto the line that depicted the game trail. "About a day's ride to the fortress. We're outside the range of their sentries tonight, but tomorrow we'll have to be more careful."

The fortress was depicted by a circle with an X through it just past the captain's finger. The trail they were on was a line going north to south. A set of narrow, parallel lines ran east to west, cutting through the mountain range between Namin and Toval, with the center depicted at the X. According to the scouts, it appeared Namin was trying to cut a second pass going through the range, with the fortress in the centermost point. The scouts hadn't been able to follow the pass all the way into Namin or back into Toval to double-check though.

"The sentries won't be a problem," someone called as a figure stepped out of the forest and walked over to join them. Captain Grall and the two soldiers standing in their circle immediately dropped hands on their swords, but Braxton held out a hand to stop them from drawing.

"Ama. I was getting worried," Braxton said to the person who joined them. "Ama is the informant who found the fortress. He's one of our best," Braxton explained to the rest of the group.

Braxton called Ama "he," but Caro wouldn't have been able to discern a gender on his own. Ama was thin and willowy, with lean muscle. Tall, but not too tall. Dark hair, dark eyes, and tanned skin, but otherwise utterly unremarkable. And yet, there was something about him. Caro studied Ama's face, trying to figure it out, as Ama pointed to the parallel lines on the map.

"This side goes all the way into Namin. It's wide enough to bring a cart through, but the road is unfinished; it's so bumpy I don't recommend bringing anything with wheels anywhere near it. They didn't completely go into Toval yet on the other side, probably to conceal what they were doing, but the path ends only a mile from the edge of the woods. It probably wouldn't be too hard to leave that last mile uncleared until after they've secured the towns in the foothills."

Braxton bent closer to follow Ama's finger, tracing along the lines on the map, and suddenly Caro saw it. They had the exact same jawline, the same bow to their lower lip. Except, Ama's brow line and the rounded turn to his nose… Caro ran his finger down the length of his own nose, feeling the same turn. Ama had blood from both the royal line of Namin and Toval; Caro was certain of it. And Braxton didn't know.

Ama looked up, saw Caro with his finger on his nose, and shook his head slightly. That head shake told Caro Ama didn't want Braxton to know. Certainly, Caro could understand why Ama wouldn't want Namin to learn he existed, but Braxton was different. Ama had to know that since he had been working as an informant for Braxton for who knew how long. Caro would keep his silence for now, but at some point, he would have to get to the bottom of the mystery that was Ama.

"Fen took his forces here," Braxton continued, oblivious to the reason for Caro's distraction. His finger went to the Tovalian side of the mountains, where Ama said the path Namin was cutting through would eventually terminate. "He'll make good time once he reaches that road. If we leave at first light, there's a fair chance we'll be inside the fortress and able to open the gates for him when he arrives not too long after us."

Captain Grall snorted. "Keep dreaming. Now tell me about those sentries," he asked Ama.

"They're lazy, and they're hungry. Closer to the fortress, this game trail follows the bottom of an old ravine with very steep walls. They figure if they camp in the middle of the ravine, no one can get past them, so they're sitting pretty as you please out in the open. If you don't mind a bit of climbing in the morning, I can show you a way to go around them."

"Is it past a spot that overlooks the fortress?" Grall asked. "That's where we went to get the lay of the place originally, but it's over a cliff face and we won't be able to get inside from there."

"That's over here," Ama said, pointing to a spot just off the game trail on the Toval side. "On this side"—he dropped his finger onto the Namin side—"is a mountain goat trail that goes almost to the fortress walls. I haven't found any evidence they're monitoring it, or that they even know it exists."

"Sloppy, but I'll take it. We'll leave the horses here in the morning and go climbing." Captain Grall rolled up the map and tucked it away. "Let's go eat." He strode off, his soldiers following in his wake. Caro, Braxton, and Ama remained behind.

"You're welcome to join us," Braxton told Ama.

"I won't turn down a hot meal," Ama replied, smiling. "Although I'm not really sure about chancing a fire so close to the fortress." He joined them in walking over toward where food was being prepared.

"It's smokeless wood, and we'll be putting it out as soon as we're done cooking," Braxton explained. "I'll see you get paid double your usual rate plus a bonus if you can get us into the fortress."

"You'll beggar yourself, then," Ama joked, grinning at them. "That's too easy. You'll see."

They joined the rest of the group for a quick dinner, then went to their bedrolls as the sun started to set, sending lengthy shadows through the trees. Caro was tired after a long day of riding, but he didn't think he was any more tired than anyone else. Alina still stopped by as he was unzipping the bedroll. Her hands glowed green briefly as she used her magic to check him.

"Right as rain," she said, patting him gently on the arm as the color faded away. "I'll leave you to get some sleep."

"How are you doing, Alina?" Caro asked, holding out a hand to stop her as she started to stand. "You didn't have to come, you know. The army has their own healers on staff."

Alina was at least ten to fifteen years older than almost everyone in their group and had spent a long time in the cushy life of the castle. This trip had to be difficult for her.

She smiled at him. "It's bringing back happy memories, to be honest. I started my healing career doing just this. I knew what I was in for, and I'm doing just fine. Thank you for your concern though." She finished standing, smiled at him again, and then walked off to wherever her bedroll was laid out. The growing gloom, exacerbated because they didn't dare keep a fire lit, allowed her to vanish from view quickly.

Caro settled into his own bedroll, zipping it closed as the nights were nippy. He was located in the center of the camp, Braxton's bedroll next to his, where they had the most protection. Shadows had lengthened into full darkness, and Caro was dozing by the time Braxton joined him. Caro rolled over and freed a hand as Braxton slid into his own bedroll. Braxton took it, squeezing tightly, and Caro didn't have to imagine his reluctance as he let go so Caro could tuck his hand back into the warmth of the depths of his bedroll.

"Sleep well," Braxton whispered, no doubt as aware as Caro that they were surrounded in all directions by eagerly listening ears and mouths all too happy to share juicy gossip.

"You too," Caro whispered back, burrowing deeper into his bedroll so the tip of his nose was covered. In the dark, salacious recesses of Caro's mind, he wanted Braxton to share a bedroll with him. Perhaps if they went camping sometime after this was all over, somewhere they didn't have a dozen soldiers and a healer escorting them, that could happen. The memory of kissing Braxton was fleeting, but, oh so sweet, and it fueled Caro's brain whenever they fell asleep so close to each other, yet still so far away. In the prior two weeks, they had both been so busy preparing for this trip they had only managed a bit of together time once, and only for about a half hour. Braxton tasted sweet, his lips soft, and his touch gentle, as if he thought Caro were a delicate piece of glass. Part of Caro desperately wanted more, to taste skin and feel firm muscle under his fingertips, and another part of Caro couldn't stand the thought, shuddering at the idea of someone touching him. Even though Braxton wasn't anything like the men who had beaten him—there was no comparison—just the thought of someone else's hands coming near him was terrifying. Which Braxton somehow understood, pulling Caro close while still maintaining some distance.

Soon, Caro hoped, the scared part of him would learn Braxton wasn't a threat. Every gentle touch, every soft caress, helped banish the lingering memories of pain and violence. Not that Caro thought those memories would magically vanish, but blunting the impact they had on his psyche with better ones would allow him to slowly return to a more normal existence. Like a simple goodnight while holding hands, which allowed Caro to finally still his thoughts and drift off into full sleep.

Chapter Eleven

THE FORTRESS WAS still being built. Caro squinted against the midmorning sun, trying to see more between the last of the colorful leaves clinging to the branches of trees looking more wintery than autumn. The reds, oranges, and mostly brown leaves hung between him and their destination, obscuring the fortress, while also hopefully helping keep them hidden. He thought they had been following a small path yesterday, but when Ama took them upward this morning, climbing into the burgeoning dawn overhead, Caro learned otherwise. The goat track Ama had discovered meandered between sturdy stones that allowed their party to climb to the top of the ridge, after which they had to practically crawl, clinging to the rocky surface and the bark of convenient trees and bushes. They couldn't have made this climb in full winter, not without the admittedly limited leaves to conceal them from any watchers below. From what Caro had heard about Toval's snow and ice, it would also probably be very slippery in a few short weeks.

Thankfully, this far to the south was still autumn, if only barely.

The fortress below them was set in another clearing, this one larger than where they had left the horses and whatever supplies they couldn't carry. The curtain wall was built, large cut stones set between natural rocky protrusions. Two gates sat at either side, where the trees had been cut for the two cart paths Caro remembered from the map. The middle portions of the fortress weren't finished. What appeared to be a large barracks building at least three stories high only had the first two floors built and the third under construction. Next to that was what appeared to be a very long stable, looking like it was going to eventually be two floors. If Caro had to guess, the second floor was likely for storage or where the servants would sleep. A third, smaller building, might be an office or mess hall, or possibly officers' quarters, but it was only foundation and no walls, so Caro couldn't make a more educated guess just yet. Right in the middle was a nine-foot by nine-foot, flat flagstone area. An uneducated observer might think it was a courtyard, stoned to keep it from turning to mud under booted feet, but Caro knew better. The space was a small arena for soldiers to fight without a proper coliseum. Disputes would end in death or severe injury in that square, all for the entertainment of others.

Caro looked away, not willing to dwell on negativity before a fight, instead trying to find some method of getting them inside. They couldn't very well open the doors when Fen arrived if they were still camped above and outside the walls.

"Sloppy. Lazy," Braxton grumbled under his breath, his voice soft so it wouldn't echo. "I see why Ama brought us up here." He looked around at the rest of the group who were all taking the same opportunity as Caro to rest after the morning's climb. "They built the wall into the mountain, and didn't add any height. From up here, we can easily climb down right into the bailey."

"I can't get an accurate count of their numbers," Grall grumbled.

People were visible below, many of them busy at work on the construction and some standing around, but Caro also couldn't tell who might be a fighter and who a civilian. Surely Namin wouldn't leave their attempt at strategic advantage unguarded, even if still under construction, but there was nowhere for an army to hide. At least, nowhere he could see from this angle.

"Right. No sense in stalling," Grall continued. "Let's go get those gates open before Prince Fen arrives. Show that bastard our scouts are just as capable as his Royal Forces," he snorted and waved briefly.

Those who had dropped down to rest stood again and walked forward, trying to remain hidden behind the leafy cover for as long as possible. The curtain wall was built of thick stones, except where it met the natural rock of the cliffs. Crouching low, scampering across the last few feet, they reached a small outcropping of cliff where there wasn't any wall to block them.

A glance downward showed cleared ground below, and they were a distance from the closest construction workers.

"Ropes," Grall hissed out, signaling with his hands.

Two men dropped bags on the ground and pulled out the thick ropes inside. They swung the end of the ropes around their waists, three full turns. Two more men stepped up. They stood in front of the trussed men, gripping the ropes tightly, but not wrapping any of it around them. The final two guards who stepped forward were smaller, but no less muscular.

Caro glanced around and saw he had missed the archers preparing their crossbows, extra arrows waiting on the ground within easy reach. The rest of the company were still crouched low, but near where they were preparing the ropes. The plan was easy enough for Caro to guess: get everyone down the ropes to the ground below as quickly as possible, with the archers providing cover from the heights. Once they were down there, the soldiers would take over and claim the fledgling building for Toval. Grall and Braxton really did want to throw the gates open to welcome Fen's arrival.

Grall waved his hands again, signing something in what Caro assumed was Toval's military shorthand. One of the people holding the rope coiled the excess at his feet, leaving only a few feet for the smaller guard, who tossed the length over the edge of the cliff. She glanced at the man with the rope around his waist, who nodded, looked at the man holding the rope, who also nodded, and she finished by obtaining Grall's nod. Permission granted, she turned her back to the cliff, gripped the rope tightly in both hands, and stepped out and over the edge, planting her feet so her body was crouched perpendicular to the cliff wall. She took one step down, her body starting to vanish from view, and then abruptly scrambled back up and over the top, landing on her knees and gesturing frantically.

Grall let out a snarl even as he waved one hand in the direction of the trees. Caro didn't need Braxton appearing at his side to understand they were retreating, although he appreciated Braxton's hand on his elbow as they reached the tree cover, and Caro promptly tripped over a rock concealed by leaf litter.

They went all the way back to the small clearing where they had been able to scout the fortress before Grall called a halt.

"Report!" Grall said, his tone soft enough not to echo but still firm.

The woman who had called for the retreat stepped forward, standing tall with her hands clasped behind her back. "They've dug out underneath the cliff, sir! A large cave, and I saw groups of soldiers resting there. I'd estimate two full flights, although I couldn't see how deep the cave went. I was more concerned with getting out of there before they spotted me."

One flight was comprised of twenty-five to fifty soldiers, depending on their specialty, which meant there were anywhere from fifty to a hundred soldiers hidden from view inside that cave, waiting for the chance to ambush anyone who might attack what appeared to be a defenseless facility. Clever. Far too clever for what Caro knew of his brother Cadell, who was supposed to be in charge of things like this.

Even fifty soldiers were too many for their band to handle. There were only twenty of them, including Caro and Alina. Caro knew how to hold a sword and fire a bow, but just barely, and he didn't know Toval's tactics or strategies well enough to fight alongside this group. His job, as Queen Trina had explained, was to watch Braxton's back. Her initial reasoning was probably more for during Braxton's more covert missions, rather than something like this, but with Caro's power he could do more to keep Braxton alive than most. Which was something Caro was definitely on board with and why he was here.

"Caro, you're frowning like this is something concerning," Braxton said when the soldier paused in her report.

Caro nodded, then shrugged. "Cadell doesn't understand subtlety, but he's in charge of all military operations for Namin. He wouldn't conceal soldiers in a cave where they had a strategic advantage; he wouldn't even think of something like this. If he had planned this, the soldiers would be camped in view because he believes the show of force would keep them from being attacked."

Plus, someone who thought to hide their fighters like this wouldn't have also left lazy sentries napping in the ravine path or a convenient overlook like this unguarded! Caro spun around, trying to see if he could spot watchers hidden in the trees. A golden glow suffused everything as he called on his magic to search.

"Don't bother, Prince Clament." The voice that rang out was familiar, but not so much that Caro could immediately place it. A second later, General Thris stepped into the clearing.

Thris was one of the top members of Namin's military, fourth or fifth after the king, although given Caro had heard some people had mysteriously fallen to their deaths from various parapets, Thris might be higher now. He wasn't alone. About thirty soldiers melted out of the forest, completely surrounding them. And yet, Caro's magic didn't sense imminent danger.

"I believe this one is yours," Thris called, waving one hand. Ama appeared through the trees a second later, walking toward them with his hands on top of his head and a wry scowl on his lips. The guard escorting him stopped at the perimeter circle, allowing Ama to continue to their group. "We've been watching him crawl all over this mountain for the last month. It's nice to know he belongs to you. Now then." His gaze slid from Caro as he switched his focus to Braxton. "I think it's time we have a little chat."

Chapter Twelve

AN ACTUAL STAIRWAY was cut into the curtain wall, allowing them to easily climb down. Ama's wry scowl had deepened into a very unhappy frown when Thris led them to it, only about a hundred yards from where they had tried to climb down with ropes. Apparently, everything Ama had learned about this fortress was only what Thris had allowed him. For a spy as competent as Braxton said Ama was, that had to rankle.

Thris pointed at the flagstone courtyard. "Wait there, please. Captain, and our two princes, if you would follow me?" He waited for Grall to join Braxton and Caro while the Naminese soldiers surrounded the rest of their small band as they went to stand in the middle of the fighting circle. Thris went into the barracks building, the rest of them following behind.

The inside was as rough and unfinished as the outside, but the office Thris led them into had a door and, inside, a long table with four chairs. He sat in one chair and waved for them to sit in the remaining three. The two

Naminese soldiers guarding them took up places inside the door, which was closed.

"You didn't take our weapons," Grall growled out, his scowl fierce, but there was a curious edge to it that matched Caro's own swirling thoughts. The three of them were still armed, hadn't been searched, and hadn't been restrained or detained in anything more than a mostly ceremonial way. Yes, they were outnumbered, but Thris knew that wouldn't stop them from fighting should an opportunity arise.

"There is little reason to," Thris replied with an easy shrug. "There is very little reason to relieve Prince—" He paused to study Braxton's face. "—Braxton, I believe, although you could be Fenwick, of his weapons. He will simply conjure more when you need them. Prince Clament only has rudimentary skills with weapons. You, Captain, I suspect are highly qualified, but you also know if you attack me now you endanger the two princes you have sworn to protect. I prefer not to waste our time with such frivolity. Don't you agree, Prince…"

"Braxton," Braxton said. "And I suspect you know exactly where Fen is right now. You want us here for something, so stop playing games."

Thris's genial smile vanished, replaced by a more serious look. He rested his elbows on the table, steepled his fingers together, and rested his chin on top.

"I suspect you already know this, Prince Clament, but your father and brother are…" He paused to search for the right word, grimacing.

"They don't think, they act, and they rely entirely on their magic to protect themselves should something go wrong," Caro filled in easily, fully aware of how asinine his family could be. "And I go by Caro now."

Thris nodded. "Since you found this fortress, I assume you know why

Namin sent us here. We're to prepare to attack Toval, and it's a way to distract the army from planning a coup."

Braxton snorted. "Sounds like the distraction isn't working."

"Oh it's not, I assure you." Thris's smile was angelic and his eyes twinkled with mischief. "Namin has been so kind to build us this stronghold in which we're protected from Namin's provocations." His mien turned more serious. "We're smuggling as many dissidents from the military out here as we can, and we're hoping the barracks will be fully habitable by winter. We're putting stores away from hunting and some gathering of nature's bounty out here, but it's going to be tight. Still, it's better than waiting to fall through ice on the pond, or to slide off a slippery tower, which is what we would all be waiting for if we stayed in Svental." He sighed. "Our plan was to amass numbers and wait through the winter, during which the rest of our citizens will have endured hunger and freezing temperatures for months, compounded with the knowledge that nothing will change in the spring because we have nothing to plant. When we attack then, we'll have full support."

"But you want to attack sooner," Braxton added, his eyes narrowed as he studied Thris.

Thris nodded, then stopped and shook his head instead. "Hundreds, if not thousands, of innocent people are going to die this winter because of the gross mismanagement of our so-called leaders. At least if we took over now, we could try to mitigate that. But we don't have the numbers to be successful right now and…" He let out another heavy sigh as he trailed off, shaking his head again.

Caro frowned. "And you don't have another ruler to instate in the king's place."

"Exactly."

Thris glanced at Caro and quickly looked away, but Caro could read between the lines even without that look. He was the bastard child and the family whipping boy. Yes, he had the royal magic, but none of the nobles whose support Caro would need as king would ever agree to stand behind him. The coup plotters needed someone else to take the throne after the coup.

Royal families all had their version of the golden-colored magic. Braxton's family could summon weapons. Caro's had the sight. Yaroi could shift into an animal form. If Namin put a king or queen on the throne without golden magic, none of the other countries would agree to trade with them, seeing them as weak. Namin would get cut off completely from the rest of the world and be in worse condition than they were now. They needed to find someone of royal Naminese blood, but that too wasn't enough. The magic was only passed down by wielders. Should Caro have children, they could be born with the magic. Caro's sister only had the barest drop of it in her; she didn't have enough power to hold the throne, and it was doubtful her future kids would be any stronger. Thris had to find another bastard like Caro, a child of King Cyphus or Prince Cadell, the only other two who could pass the power down, and then put them on the throne.

A thorny issue without an answer. Caro rubbed his fingers across his forehead, hoping to stave off the budding headache he could feel building, and then rubbed downward over his nose so he could rest his chin on his palm. But…his fingers stopped on his nose as an idea came to him.

"If numbers are an issue, the majority of the Tovalian army should arrive by this evening," Braxton was saying as Caro slowly dropped his hand into his lap. "If it means removing the constant threat on our border from Namin, we would be happy to aid in deposing your king. I don't know if I can help with finding you a new one though."

"Ask Ama," Caro blurted out, then clamped his mouth shut.

Thris only looked at Caro curiously, but the way Braxton's face went blank said maybe he did know the truth about Ama. Or at least he suspected. Whether Ama actually knew anyone in his family with the golden power who might qualify was a question, but there was a chance.

"I'll ask," Braxton replied before turning back to Thris. "Either way, King Cyphus cannot remain on the throne. Your people will be so grateful to have the food and grain Toval will lend you this winter; they won't mind the regent you appoint doesn't have golden magic. That will give you at least a year or two to find someone before the international community starts to take note. We can hash out the finer details when Fen arrives."

Thris nodded slowly as his frown smoothed. "Right. We will definitely ask for Prince Fenwick's opinion, but I believe it's fair to say we have the beginnings of a plan. I will send word to my operatives in the city to expect our arrival. Which only leaves the thorny issue of how to get close enough to the king and prince fast enough that their magic won't have time to warn them."

There were no doubts or worries about betraying his birth family in Caro's mind as he opened his mouth and said, "I can help with that."

Chapter Thirteen

"THE WAY OUR passive magic works is it identifies threats in time for us to move to a safe location." The firelight flickered over people's faces, barely visible in the dark, but they were all listening intently. Braxton sat on Caro's left, Fen just past him. The rest of the group were the people tasked with infiltrating the royal apartments and capturing or killing King Cyphus and Prince Cadell. "If your intent is to take your belt knife and stab me, and you're thinking about doing just that, my magic will warn me. The important bit is *when* the magic warns me. If you're two rooms away and thinking about stabbing me, then I have the length of time it will take for you to traverse those rooms to flee. If you start thinking about it right now, when you're five feet away, I might have enough warning to dodge, but not enough to escape ahead of time. That means you cannot even think about harming one of us until you're close enough to strike or you'll never get close enough."

"Damn," Grall said, groaning. "My pre-battle mental focus would ruin our plot completely."

"Mine too," Thris admitted. "How do we get around that magic?"

"And isn't talking about it right now going to warn them?" Fen added, glancing to his left, across the field of low brush and grass where they were camping, toward the direction of where Svental was located only a few miles away.

Caro shook his head. "There's an outer limit to our power. Otherwise, we would never get any peace. I promise you, my father and brother likely think about killing me regularly, and I didn't notice until the assassins were in the castle in Etoval about two minutes away. Like I said when we were planning this, I can guide you through the secret passages." In fact, the plan was based heavily on Namin's most recent attempt at killing the Tovalian royal family, minus the poisoning, of course. Caro's group would copy their use of the secret passages to sneak into the royal chambers and get close to King Cyphus and Prince Cadell. "What we need to do is think innocent thoughts as we approach. How nice the walls look or how clean the floors are. Sing a song in your head or think about the good you're doing to support Toval and Namin. When you draw your weapon, only think that you're checking to see how shiny it is. One stray thought about *killing* them could ruin it."

"Tough not to think about why we're creeping up on them," Thris said, frowning. "But if that's the only way to actually win, we'll have to succeed. Is there any other way they might notice us?"

"Only if they actively call on their magic." Caro shrugged. "When I'm using my magic, I can see through walls and hear conversations in other rooms. But only when I'm actively using it or I'm alerted to a threat. It's not something automatic, otherwise. As long as we're quiet and thinking inno-cent thoughts, we shouldn't have any issues."

Thris let out a heavy sigh, but a moment later, he grinned. "Right. We're going to have some fun tomorrow. We leave as soon as it's light enough for the horses, so let's get some shut-eye." He clapped his hands on his knees and stood, then ambled off toward his bedroll.

Caro also thought it was time to try getting some sleep. He stood as well, and Braxton, who so far had only been a supporting presence at Caro's side, joined him. They walked together toward where they, Fen, and Char had laid out their bedrolls. Char would remain behind at this camp with Alina and the handful of other supporting staff but had cooked for them the last few nights as they traveled through Namin. Caro wasn't certain he would ever be able to eat regular food again.

His bedroll was exactly as he left it. Caro sat on top of it to take off his boots, but paused midway through loosening the laces to let out a heavy sigh.

"You going to be okay tomorrow?" Braxton asked, settling onto the bedroll next to him.

Caro sighed again. "My father and brother earned everything coming to them, and considering how they treated me, it's almost poetic that I'm the one leading their doom to their doorstep. Just…" He shrugged, unsure how to put all the thoughts swirling through his head into words.

"They're your only family. Even if they are terrible people, we're still talking about killing your father and your brother."

"I don't love them. I don't even like them," Caro said, trying to ex-plain but mostly relieved Braxton had yet again divined his thoughts and helped Caro get them out in the open.

"But that doesn't mean they don't hold some level of import to you, even if it's in the role of a bogeyman." Braxton wrapped his arm over Caro's shoulders and pulled him into a hug. "If you weren't finding this difficult, I would be concerned."

Caro tried to relax into Braxton's embrace, into the warmth and comfort he exuded. He tried to still his mind, pushing every worry and fear to the background, but he failed. The night surrounding them was soothing, at least. Darkness, punctuated by stars far overhead, gave the illusion that they were home in Etoval, sitting in the royal garden on top of the palace. Now they were done talking, and the crickets and frogs had resumed chirping, until it seemed as if Caro and Braxton were the only two people for miles around.

It was only when Braxton gently shook him awake, revealing the first hints of dawn just beginning to glow low on the horizon, that Caro realized he had somehow managed to fall asleep. Braxton pressed a warm bowl into Caro's hands, and after blinking blearily at it for a long minute, Caro realized it was full of oatmeal.

"Eat up. Once everyone's ready, we'll head out."

Caro obeyed, and even though his stomach immediately soured at the memory of where they were going and why, one spoonful of Char's cooking led to an empty bowl far too quickly. Horses were being saddled when Caro went over to the kitchen area to return the bowl, and he found Fen and Char holding hands and looking far too ooey-gooey for such an early hour.

"You'll be safe?" Fen asked Char as Caro hurried to locate the drop-off spot for dirty dishes.

Char nodded. "As soon as you're gone, we'll pack up camp and head out too. The big trading city of Talvn is a couple miles that way," he added, pointing south. "That's where I completed my apprenticeship after school, so I know the area well, and I have friends who will help. I'll hide there until we get word to come meet you."

Caro scurried away as Fen bent to take a kiss, glad to find his horse and Braxton, and to disappear amid the bustle of the soldiers around him.

"Right!" Thris called, clapping his hands to bring everyone to order. "You all know the plan. Last night, the majority of our forces snuck into the city, where they are ready to attack the castle from multiple gates as loudly as possible. We won't know whether they will only serve as a distraction for us, whether they'll be able to breech the gates, or whether any townspeople will join in or fight back. Either way, we need to be inside the castle before they begin. Remember, from here on out, the only thing you should be thinking about is how this is a lovely day to go visit grandma. One stray thought of our real objective could ruin it all. But you soldiers are the best of the best. That's why you were hand-picked to be here! We are going to go kick ass and take back our country from the tyrant running it!"

The answering roar startled a few roosting birds, who flew off chirping indignantly.

"Mount up!" Thris finished, putting words to action as he slid a foot into the high stirrup of his horse and heaved himself into the saddle. Caro obeyed, climbing onto his own horse.

Thris rode over to Caro, stopping at his side and waiting patiently as Caro got the reins situated.

"Right. Show us the way to the hidden entrance."

Caro grabbed onto his resolve and nodded firmly. "This way." He walked his horse through the crowd until he was in the lead, then settled into a ground-eating trot on the path to destroying his past and hopefully ensuring his future.

Chapter Fourteen

THE PATH TO his own bedroom through the secret passages was forefront in Caro's mind. The various turns and hallways he had used for years to hide from the public eye, and thereby preventing any of his family from noticing him, were all he thought about as he walked through the far-too-familiar pathways up until the moment when Caro stopped outside the one doorway he had never dared use before. He refocused his thoughts on the lock, which was a deadbolt-style that required multiple turns of the knob to pull back. Preventing the bar from scraping or the knob from squeaking was all he allowed himself to worry about. Once the door was unlocked, he took a step back and to the side, motioning Thris forward with a wave of his arm.

Thris drew his sword, echoed by the rest of their group, before waving for another soldier to yank the door open.

They fell into the king's sitting room with a roar, dashing forward into an immediate melee. Caro followed, staying back and out of the way. He was fully aware he wasn't nearly as well trained as the mixture of Thris, Fen, and Braxton's elite fighters. Caro remained by the secret door, ready to join the fighting should he be needed, though he hoped that wouldn't be necessary.

Four guards were always stationed by the door in the king's private rooms. The king also had two bodyguards with him at all times. The crown prince had an additional two bodyguards, and Prince Cadell was also properly trained in how to use a sword. This time of the morning, Cadell and King Cyphus ate breakfast together. Caro had never been certain whether Cadell was getting trained as heir, or whether it was Cyphus's way of monitoring him to prevent Cadell from stealing the throne early. Caro had certainly never been invited to dine with them. What that meant was nine fighters immediately jumped to their feet to engage with the fighters coming out of the hidden door, and their shouts brought more guards from the hallway.

Swords clanged, and fighters grunted and yelled. Furniture screeched as it was shoved out of the way, and dishes clattered as the breakfast table was overturned. Cadell was yelling about something as he was surrounded by fighters from both sides, including Fen and Thris, but Caro couldn't make out the words over the rest of the cacophony. Braxton was on the other side of the room, part of a group fighting over there.

Once the initial influx of guards from the hallway had ended, Caro expected more to arrive from the barracks or other hallways. That was why their plan was to take out King Cyphus and Prince Cadell quickly, and escape back into the secret passages to join the rest of the fighters in the city. But the doorway remained empty. Namin had about fifteen people fighting for them, against Caro's group of thirty. The outcome was decided.

Only… Caro sucked in a breath, his gaze casting around the room and trying and failing to find the familiar, hated face of his father, King Cyphus. There was no sign of graying blond hair or angry blue eyes, or even a spot where he could be hiding. His bodyguards were here, fighting, which meant he had to be in residence. But he was definitely not in the sitting room.

Perhaps their attack had happened a few minutes too early, and King Cyphus hadn't yet emerged from his rooms to have breakfast with Cadell. Or, they had failed to conceal their approach from Cyphus's magic, and he had fled. Either way, they had to find him or the coup would fail.

Since the guards from the hallway outside hadn't rushed in until after the fighting began, Caro felt it safe to assume King Cyphus hadn't fled that way. Additionally, Prince Cadell had been left like a sitting duck when he could have fled after King Cyphus had Cyphus gone out that way if he did indeed flee. King Cyphus might not care overly much about anything but his own comforts and security, but Cadell was the only viable heir in Namin. Losing Cadell would destabilize Cyphus's rule and reduce their international standing. Not having an heir in Namin could cause absolute chaos. Other countries wouldn't want to continue even the already limited trade agreements they had with Namin. Had he the chance, King Cyphus would have fled with Cadell in tow. Which meant King Cyphus had to be in the private bedroom area of the royal apartment.

Braxton must have come to the same conclusion since he was fighting his way toward the doorway that led deeper into the apartment. And yet, an alarm went off at the back of Caro's brain. Perhaps King Cyphus thought his fighters could win against the invading force, but would he really trust them? Fleeing into a dead end would only increase his chances of getting caught. Unless…

A terrible scream interrupted Caro's swirling thoughts. He spun to look and let out a squeaking gasp. Cadell hung off Thris's sword, impaled like a bug in the museum's curio collection. The sword had pierced through his stomach, at an upward angle with the tip penetrating out his back near his shoulder blade. Cadell's heart must have been skewered.

Cadell twitched once before going limp, and Thris twisted his sword as he lowered his arm to ensure the damage was permanent. Cadell's body hit the floor with a thud that seemed to echo in Caro's mind, the sneering lips and condescending eyes replaced by the slackness of death. The older boy who had broken Caro's arm in a fit of rage when Caro was six; the young man who had used the younger Caro as a practice dummy when he was learning sword fighting; and the prince who had ordered Caro to join a mercenary band in a doomed attempt to invade Toval—knowing Caro likely wouldn't survive—lay there like a mannequin, blood pooling beneath him onto the cream-colored carpet. Dead. Gone. The boogeyman of Caro's childhood, the terror of Caro's adult life, and the only older brother he'd ever had was gone. Caro let out a breath he hadn't realized he'd been holding, the violent exhalation masked under the roar as the coup forces were galvanized, and the Namin defenders fought to protect what was left of the royal family.

Reminded, and glad for the distraction if he was being honest, Caro spun and dashed back into the secret passage. King Cyphus wouldn't box himself into a corner. No, there had to be a second exit into the secret passages from the bedroom area.

Caro's fears were immediately validated. Light shown into the dark hallway from a second open door a few feet down from where Caro was standing. A flicker of moment caught Caro's attention, and he looked up just in time to see the trailing hem of a dressing gown vanish around a corner ahead.

"He's getting away!" Caro yelled into the sitting room, but his legs were already moving. Caro took off down the passageway, hoping some of the soldiers would follow as he tried to catch up to the fleeing king. He slid around the corner just in time to see a foot disappear around a left-hand turn, and when he reached that corner Caro saw a flash of graying blond hair—King Cyphus's back as he descended a staircase. Caro was catching up. Eyes on the prize, he scampered down the stairs, arriving at a landing with a hallway heading left and right as well as the switchback for more stairs. King Cyphus couldn't have gotten so far ahead that Caro wouldn't see him down the hall, so Caro took the stairs. Twice more, Caro reached a landing and had to continue downward, following what he hoped was the king's path into the depths of the castle until he finally reached the bottom level, and his only option was to try the hallway.

The mage lights were out in this hall. Caro squinted through the gloom, trying to still his panting breaths so he could listen for any noise ahead. He crept forward slowly, looking to both sides and straining his ears for the slightest noise to indicate where the king had gone. He didn't dare call up his magic to search; he might be able to pinpoint where the king was hiding, but the glow would give away his own position far faster. He inched his way forward, trying to sense some clue as to where the king had gone.

A sudden clatter off to Caro's right, like the sound of several items falling to the floor, had Caro turning in that direction. A second clatter and a muffled curse and Caro hurried his steps. He passed through an opening of some sort, the solid edges dark in the gloom, as he followed a third, muffled, clanking noise.

And then the thud of a door closing and *thunk* of a heavy bar dropping to lock it echoed in what Caro realized was a rather small room. The limited light immediately vanished, leaving Caro standing in complete darkness, trapped.

Interlude

BRAXTON WIPED SWEAT, blood, and other substances off his face with a handkerchief. He had made the mistake of trying to wipe with the back of his hand far too many times in previous battles, and scraping the skin off his nose with the armored edge of his vambraces wasn't something he wanted to do today. The room was a disaster. Blood had splattered everywhere, punctuated by the bodies lying where they had fallen. Fen stood over the final two guards, who had surrendered and sat against the far wall. Thris called out orders to the soldiers tearing apart the royal apartments, searching for the king. Grall leaned against one of the overturned couches, his own handkerchief up as he attempted to stymie a bloody nose. And Caro…

Braxton cast around, searching for a head of bright, blond hair and coming up empty. Braxton searched among the bodies, his heart in his mouth at what he'd find before finally letting out a sigh of relief when there was no sign of Caro.

"Has anyone seen Caro?" Braxton called, heading through the doorway into the lavish, garish bedroom. Nearly every surface was gold, from the gilded walls and furniture, to all the decorations. Even the bedding was stitched with gold thread. Braxton wondered how that could even be comfortable; he had to squint to keep from being blinded. Caro's hair might have blended in with the general theme, but he definitely wasn't there or in the attached dressing and washing rooms either. Braxton returned to the sitting room to look again.

"Make sure to preserve this body," Fen explained to some of the soldiers. He was reorganizing their group post-battle, moving bodies out of the way to prevent them from becoming a tripping hazard should the room become another battlefield. "We need to display him somehow, to reassure the people their tyrant prince is no more."

"Has anyone seen Caro?" Braxton repeated. He only received headshakes in reply.

"He yelled something over by the doorway around when the prince was killed," Grall said, his words muffled by the handkerchief pressed to his nose. "But I had my hands full at the time, so I don't know what."

Braxton nodded his thanks and headed for the secret doorway, stepping out into the hallway, heart sinking when he didn't immediately find Caro. What he did find was a pool of light emanating from a second open door a few feet down the hall. Braxton jogged over, peeking in to find a screen of clothing. He shoved the clothes aside and grimaced at the shocked exclamations from Thris's soldiers searching the king's closet on the other side.

"My guess is the king escaped this way," he said to the group who had turned to look at him. Caro had followed the king. Braxton was certain of that. But Caro wasn't… Braxton cut that thought off before it could grow. Caro knew basic sword work and his body was healed, but he hadn't yet had the time to build up his endurance. If the king was proficient in fighting, he could likely overpower Caro far too easily, but Braxton halted his thoughts again. He wasn't going there. Besides, Caro had extremely powerful magic that as far as Braxton had been able to tell was actually stronger than his father's or his brother's had been. A lot of the problems Caro had told Braxton about from his childhood came down to how damned jealous his family was of him.

Braxton returned to the sitting room. "We need to organize a search of the castle. The king escaped from a second door and it looks like Caro went after him."

"We need to know how the rest of our allies are faring first, unfortunately," Thris replied with a grimace full of frustration. They had really hoped to catch both the king and prince in their one attack. Now the king had a chance to regroup while they were stuck in place, waiting.

Braxton went over to one of the windows, looking out into the early morning sunlight as it bathed the lush garden below. Everything looked serene, far different to the blood-soaked nightmare behind him and the anxious thudding in his heart over Caro being missing. However, as he watched a plume of black smoke billowed past, blowing on a breeze that danced between the trees and bushes below.

"Something's definitely on fire out there, so they're doing something."

Before anyone could respond, the sounds of booted feet running on carpet, a muffled *thud, thud,* came from the outside hallway where the double doors into the suite were thrown open.

"Coming to report!" someone yelled.

The white flash of Fen's teeth as he grinned was all Braxton needed to drop his grip on his sword hilt and relax, but the rest didn't relax until Fen called out a response.

"Jensen, get your ass in here!"

Fen's second in command, Jensen, entered the room with one of Thris's men at his side. They both saluted, and thankfully Jensen began to explain without any more fanfare.

"Our simultaneous attack on all three gates was successful. The western gate had deteriorated, exactly as General Thris said, so we were able to make entry into the outer bailey quickly and get the other two gates open. The majority of the soldiers surrendered, especially when they saw the coup fighters also wore Namin uniforms. There is some reactionary rioting in the city, and as you also predicted, we ended up with a supporting force of shopkeepers and laborers helping from the rear as soon as word got out that we were here. There were a handful of areas in the bailey where fighting was serious. Captain Zain believes she took out the Triumviré barracks, which housed the most difficult fighters. Their building caught fire too, which helped us. She sent us to report while she finishes the remaining cleanup."

"Excellent work," Fen replied with a firm nod. "General Thris, the castle and country are yours. How would you like to proceed?"

Thris stepped forward. "We need to find the king before that is actually true. I want a full, systematic search of the castle conducted. I want all servants brought to the servant dining hall, and all nobles brought to the throne room. Aside from our soldiers, no one should be allowed elsewhere. We will find the king and Prince Caro, and bring an end to the rule of kleptocracy."

Jensen and Thris's man saluted again before leaving. Zain would absolutely ensure no stone went unturned from her end in the search party. Now that they knew the castle was secured, it was time for Braxton to start his own search. Caro was somewhere inside this damned castle, and Braxton was going to find him. No matter how long it took.

Chapter Fifteen

CARO STOOD IN the dark, completely frozen in place, his heart thudding frantically. He couldn't see the end of his nose, let alone anything else; the darkness was absolute. He was certain he had made a major mistake and gotten himself locked into a room of some sort as a prisoner or a hostage. After what felt like forever, a flare of light lit the room, giving him a chance to get his bearings. He was in what appeared to be an empty storeroom, five foot square and built completely of solid stone. A small window set into the door at head height was open, revealing perfectly functional mage lights in the hallway. Caro had definitely, stupidly, walked right into a trap.

King Cyphus appeared in the window, blocking the light with his smarmy smirk. "You and your nasty little friends have failed. Spectacularly failed." He laughed, but his eyes were cold and sharp, calculating as he looked at Caro. "I'll have this castle back to rights by nightfall, and every single one of them will be publicly beheaded, especially the damned bastards from Toval. And you will watch as every head rolls, knowing you won't receive the luxury of a quick death. Oh no. For your betrayal, I will ensure yours is slow and incredibly painful."

He was overconfident and boasting, with zero idea of who was actually part of the coup, Caro quickly realized. Toval might have joined Namin, but there was no way whatever was left of the king's supporters would ever be able to best Braxton and Fen. Plus, if King Cyphus had fled from his bedroom, he likely didn't know about their second, larger group invading the castle from the city.

"Prince Cadell is dead," Caro replied, affecting an unconcerned shrug and hoping to enrage King Cyphus enough to perhaps make his own mistake. Caro might be locked up, but he was locked up with all his weapons. If he could dupe King Cyphus into unlocking that door, it was over. "You have no heir, and aside from me, the only other of your children to inherit the royal magic is Cybill, and she can barely even see imminent danger. She has no ability to see the present and therefore cannot rule this country. Without an heir, Namin is destroyed. The coup was successful."

King Cyphus's eyes narrowed and his lips thinned as anger set in, but then he gave his own unconcerned shrug, and his expression settled into his usual nasty smirk. "Do you have any idea how easy it would be to make a new heir? Women beg me for attention. They'll be lining up in droves for the chance to bear the next heir to the throne."

Caro scoffed, purposefully imparting as much disbelief as he could into the sound. "Please. The official report said she was sick, but we all know Cadell's mother took her own life. My mother only begged for you to leave her alone. Cybill's mother fled to another country. The list of women who couldn't wait to escape you is far longer. Besides, you're an old, decrepit waste of a human being. I doubt you have any virility left."

King Cyphus let out a snarl full of rage and slammed the window shut, plunging Caro back into darkness. Caro waited, hand on his sword hilt, hoping to hear the thud of the bar being removed from the door. Long seconds passed, each feeling like an eon, but he heard nothing. Disappointed his idea had failed, Caro let out a sigh and sat down, the floor hard, cold stone under his butt.

He knew he was a fool. Running off without any sort of backup, with no way of anyone knowing where he had gone or why. He ought to have let the king flee, and then once he had a group gathered, used his magic to find him again. There was no need to sprint through the secret passages like Caro had, but some sort of battle madness had clearly taken him over. He hadn't been thinking, just reacting, and now he was stuck in a dark hole until either rescue arrived or King Cyphus decided to kill him.

Self-recrimination wasn't going to get him anywhere. And there unfortunately wasn't anything he could actually do to escape. However, he could use his magic to see what was going on elsewhere, and perhaps gather information he could throw at the king the next time he wanted to chat in order to enrage him enough to open that door. It was worth a shot and certainly better than sitting in the dark beating himself up. Caro let out a breath and released his magic, suffusing the room in a golden glow as his third eye opened. He pushed, sending his consciousness out, away from his body. He closed his physical eyes and looked with his magical ones instead.

The hallway outside his cell was empty, no sign of the king or anyone else. Caro pushed farther out into the castle proper, which was teeming with people. Soldiers in groups of four, mixed groups wearing both the uniforms of Namin and Toval, were going door-to-door and room-to-room, and anyone they found was being gathered into a group and brought to either the throne room or one of the large servant's halls. Some of the nobles were definitely less than enthused to be woken before noon and dragged out of their comfortable suites in their bedclothes. Lots of shouting, and a few were struggling, but the soldiers didn't bend. Every room was emptied and every person delivered to their meeting location. The beautiful, powerful woman Caro had met once, Captain Patricia Zain, stood in the entrance hall, giving out orders and listening to reports, her fierce scowl shutting down any arguments from the nobles being guided past her before they could start.

Caro didn't see Braxton though. He directed his magic and zoomed through the halls in the direction of the royal wing, although he bypassed it and went into the secret passages. Thankfully, he found Braxton after only a few moments of searching. Braxton's forehead was wrinkled in concentration, a deep V lowering his brows, but he looked determined and somehow even more beautiful than usual. He was part of a team of four exploring the hallway one story down from the royal apartment. Curious, Caro went up one flight to find Fen with his own group, exploring the cross hallway there.

"I think these passages might run through the entire castle," Fen groaned out to one of his group members. "Hopefully, we'll get more searchers soon!"

"As soon as they finish clearing the actual castle, I'm sure Zain will send more groups our way," one of the men with Fen replied. Caro recognized him, but could only remember his name started with an R.

While their conversation was interesting, Caro much preferred to watch Braxton. He directed his magic to return to Braxton's group.

"I'll bet there are secret doors hidden all along these walls," one of Braxton's group members was saying when Caro reached them again. "There's no telling what we might be missing behind them, but figuring out how to open each door would be impossible!"

"Thris seemed certain that any of the hidden doors led into actual rooms in the castle, which the other groups are searching. We might run into someone trying to escape this way, but we don't need to open each door ourselves," one of the other group members added.

The line between Braxton's brows only deepened. The group continued on until they reached what appeared to be a dead end. The hidden door to one of the extra-large meeting rooms was there, but required knowing how to use a complicated lever to open it.

"Right. Let's search the other side of the landing now," Braxton said, turning and leading the group back down the hallway.

Caro clenched his teeth, desperately wishing he could reach out and grab Braxton and drag him down two flights of stairs and through the hall to the door with a bar locking it. Unfortunately, his magic only allowed looking, not touching. As frustrating as it might be, Caro was glad he at least knew Braxton was coming. He leaned his physical body against the wall in his cell to conserve energy and followed Braxton with his magic as he returned to the staircase and continued onward down the other side of the hall.

Minutes inched by, moving as quickly as a slug climbing a hill. Caro watched Braxton, his face pinched with worry and his eyes blazing with anger, and Caro relaxed. Braxton wouldn't stop searching until he found Caro, and he was moving in the right direction. Only two floors to go, and Caro would be freed again. Of course, Braxton had to find Caro before the king returned, but Caro felt it safe to assume if the king knew search parties were looking through the secret passages, he would hide elsewhere. At least, Caro hoped that was the case.

Braxton was nearing the secret door Caro used to get into his small bedroom here in the castle, about halfway down this particular secret passage, when his magic suddenly flared. Gold flashed against the stone walls of his cell as Caro gasped and opened his eyes, jumping to his feet and dropping a hand on his sword hilt. He cast around the room, but didn't see anything different. He didn't hear anything happening outside the cell door either.

Caro gritted his teeth and tried to get his magic under control. He wanted to thrust it out, past the cell door to see where the danger was, but it slipped out of his control like water sliding between his fingers. And yet, strangely, the magic didn't feel like a warning of danger. He didn't have the normal feeling of panic or imminent attack in the focus. Rather, the magic seemed to be flaring with joy, as if it was a warning of welcome, which had never happened before.

"Is something good coming?" Caro asked aloud.

The magic flared one last time, bright and eye-searing, before finally settling as if expressing its pleasure that Caro understood its message. Since his own magic wasn't supposed to be sentient, Caro swallowed hard. Still, the magic was designed to provide advanced warning, so maybe this was merely another aspect of it that had been forgotten. Or, more likely, that Caro had never been taught, since once he had gained control over the basics, the lessons had abruptly ended. Caro had always suspected he was magically the strongest of all his siblings, but the unwanted bastard could never be heir. By refusing to teach him, they prevented Caro from appearing to be stronger than Cadell. Although, Caro had only realized that in hindsight. At the time, losing those lessons had just compounded the hurt of everything else he had been enduring.

"Okay," Caro said, closing his eyes and focusing on his magic. "What do you want to show me?"

The magic yanked his consciousness away, relentlessly tugging him through the castle and all the way to the main entrance courtyard outside. Sometime in the last hour, Captain Zain had moved out there and was currently scowling at two people riding in through the gate on horseback.

"Who are you and how did you get past the guards?" Zain's voice boomed loud enough to be heard even over all the commotion, bringing the noise to an abrupt halt as everyone turned to look at the newcomers.

The taller of the two held out one empty hand. Green magic flared for a brief moment, before solidifying over that hand in the shape of the seal of Toval.

"I showed them this," they replied. A deep hood covered the head, concealing any facial features, and the voice was androgynous, but Caro was certain Ama was the one speaking. At Braxton's request, Ama had gone in search of a new ruler for Namin, someone who had the royal magic and who could take over as ruler of the country once the coup was complete. At the time, Ama's face had gone suspiciously blank, as if he was concealing some sort of raging thoughts. His only response was, "I'll see what I can do," and the next morning he had vanished from the fortress.

That he had arrived so quickly, and with a companion, hopefully meant he was successful. Caro eagerly turned his attention to the smaller person. She had her hood up as well, but it draped over her curves enough to reveal her gender. And then graceful hands lifted, gripped the edge, and lowered the hood.

Golden blonde hair and brilliant blue eyes shone, and Caro's gasp was echoed by many of the people in the courtyard. She looked to be in her late thirties or early forties, but from her looks, she could very easily have been Caro's sister or aunt. The blood relation was blatant to anyone who had ever even glimpsed a member of the Namian royal family.

"My name is Carmillian, and I am the rightful Queen of Namin, returned from exile now that the false king has been removed from his stolen throne," she called out, her voice clear and ringing. Her smile was gentle and full of understanding as she looked around at everyone assembled in the courtyard. "I don't expect you to simply believe me, so let me prove it to you, for I am the true All-Seeing, the true All-Knowing. The past, present, and future all bare their secrets to me as they did to the rightful kings and queens of old." Golden magic flared, and her third eye opened in the center of her forehead. The light grew and grew, until it was almost blinding in intensity. Even Caro's spirit body squinted through the glare. As it finally started to dim, she turned and looked in the direction of where Caro hovered.

"Cousin," she said, although her physical lips didn't move. Somehow, she was able to project her voice through her magic, something Caro certainly hadn't known was possible. "I see you are in a bit of a predicament. I will come free you immediately, so please do not continue to overtax yourself unnecessarily."

As if mentioning it was the trigger, Caro could suddenly feel the pull from his physical body and the tired ache that spoke of magic overuse. He didn't know if it was actually true, but he was once told if he wasn't careful, he could accidentally sever the connection between spirit and body. When the magic called him back, he had to obey.

Caro's last glimpse of Carmillian and the courtyard was the golden glow fading as she closed her third eye, and a brief glance of everyone wearing Namin colors on their knees, bowing. And then his spirit snapped back into his body, and all he could see was the hint of stone walls through the darkness in the room. Caro sat again, slumping against the wall in exhaustion. He had definitely overextended, and Alina was going to be very unhappy with him, but Caro was happy all the same. Rescue was coming, either Braxton or Carmillian would reach him soon, and Carmillian appeared to be a much better prospective ruler than King Cyphus had ever actually been. Satisfied with the day—even despite his stupidity in getting trapped in the first place—Caro was happy to close his eyes and let his magical exhaustion pull him into sleep.

Chapter Sixteen

"HE'S HERE!" CARMILLIAN'S voice was powerful and full of authority, the sound immediately dragging Caro from sleep and back into reality. The scraping thud of the bar being removed banished the last of his sleepy lethargy, so he jumped to his feet as the door was yanked open.

Bright light from the hallway outside flooded the room, blinding him.

"Caro!"

Hearing Braxton calling his name was the best thing that had happened to Caro that day. Caro stumbled forward, blinking away the stars clouding his vision, and found himself suddenly enveloped in familiar, welcoming, and so-very-warm arms. Caro gripped the front of the tunic covering Braxton's armor, wishing he could press closer and feel skin against skin and listen to Braxton's heartbeat, which Caro presumed was thumping as hard as Caro's. Since he couldn't do that, he tucked his nose into the side of Braxton's neck, where the shoulder of his armor ended, accessible thanks to the fact that Braxton had removed his helmet, and breathed in the scent of sweat, man, and Braxton. For the first time since the decision had been made to attack the castle in Svental, Caro's shoulders relaxed and he finally felt he could breathe.

"Cousin," Carmillian said softly, as if she regretted the necessity of needing to interrupt.

Caro reluctantly pulled away but was gratified when Braxton immediately took his hand. "Queen Carmillian Svent, it is an honor to meet you," Caro replied, bowing low.

"No need for that, cousin," she replied, reaching out with one hand to motion him back upright. "You were instrumental in aiding with the removal of the false king and helping me return to my rightful place. You will never need to bow to me."

Caro had a ton of questions, number one being the fact that he had zero living aunts or uncles and definitely no cousins. His father had been very efficient in removing any potential competition. Yet, the fact that Carmillian clearly had the royal power gave her the right to claim the throne. If she was a better ruler than King Cyphus, Caro didn't have any issues. He just didn't know how they were related or even where she had come from. Now wasn't the time or place to ask, though, so Caro kept his mouth shut.

"While Prince Caro's sentiments are appreciated, before I can officially be called queen, we first need to locate the impostor king," she continued. "He is knowledgeable enough in the use of Namin's royal magic to conceal himself from other royals, so I cannot locate him as I did Caro. Prince Braxton, please continue your search. He must be somewhere in this castle, so you or one of the other groups will find him eventually. I believe it is time for me to address the residents of this castle, the servants and the nobles whom you have confined. Prince Caro, would it be possible for you to accompany me?"

Caro squeezed Braxton's hand, and Braxton squeezed back. They could go their separate ways for now to do their duty as princes of their respective kingdoms, safe in the knowledge that when their tasks were complete, they would be together again.

"I would be happy to join you," Caro replied, but then he glanced down at what he was wearing, which was armor covered by a travel-stained tunic in the colors of Toval, same as Braxton's. "Should I put on a more appropriate outfit first?" He probably had some suitable clothes stashed in his bedroom.

Carmillian frowned in thought for a moment before shaking her head. "No. It will hammer in the point that things have changed if you show up as you are." She grinned. "I bet some of your detractors will be eating crow."

She knew about his past. Ama had likely told her, or she might actually be able to see the past like she claimed and had taken a look into his history. That was good, since it meant she was prepared for how little having his support would mean.

"I doubt it, but if you want me there, I'm happy to support you."

"Right." She clapped her hands. "Let's get to work."

The groups dispersed, Braxton slowly released Caro's hand, squeezing one last time before he returned to the hallway he had been searching before Carmillian had waylaid him. Caro led the way for Carmillian, Ama, and the small group of soldiers he assumed Captain Zain had assigned to guard her—or, more likely, to keep watch on her to ensure she wasn't a snake like the rest of Caro's family. Caro was therefore the only one who actually knew the passages.

"Do you want to see the nobles or the servants first?" Caro asked when they had climbed two sets of stairs and had paused to catch their breath on the landing.

"Nobles first. Before they riot because they weren't able to sleep off last night's hangovers, haven't been served breakfast, and were forced into public in their night robes." She giggled. "Toval's Captain Zain has a bit of a mean streak, one I heartily approve of."

"She just doesn't take any nonsense," Caro replied. He might have only met her once, but he was certain she wasn't mean-spirited, just direct and unwilling to allow fools to get their selfish whims. He led the way down the hall to the right, waving at Fen's group as they passed. The throne room had a small antechamber behind the throne, a place where accoutrements of state could be stored for use throughout the day and retrieved with ease. It also hid the secret door. From the outside, the door required Caro push a button, which released a lever that had to be pulled down until it was completely flat, to release the lock. One of the guards went through first to check the room and waved them forward a moment later. Caro followed Carmillian inside, waited for the rest of their group to follow, and then closed the door again.

"Through there is the dais where the throne sits," he explained when Carmillian craned her neck, trying to see outside of the tiny room without actually sticking her head out. "It's illegal for anyone not invited by the king to even touch the dais, so everyone will be on the floor about three feet below. Guards will be stationed around the room, but they'll be handpicked by Captain Zain and shouldn't be a problem."

She nodded at him. "Right. That helps. Let's do this."

Carmillian straightened her shoulders and strode forward, out onto the dais with her head held high. Caro followed, one step back and to her left as the second most important person in her entourage. The rest of the group ranged behind them, spreading out along the back wall as Carmillian came to a stop about a foot from the edge.

The room was rectangular, with the dais at one end and massive doors currently closed and guarded at the other. The assembled nobles were actually in their dressing robes. Caro had thought that a joke, but Zain had literally dragged them out of bed without a chance to primp and pamper. Which meant they were furious and anxious. Haughty nobles didn't look nearly as snobbish when they were half naked, and their sneers down their noses fell flat. Although, most of them gasped, surprise on their faces rather than sneers, when they caught sight of Carmillian. The room fell silent as heads turned in her direction.

"My good people of Namin, you have been lied to for the last time!" Carmillian called, her voice again containing that authoritative note that made Caro immediately want to trust her, as if she was so certain of her words being true that the chances of there being another interpretation were nonexistent. "The false king is finally gone, and the rightful heir has returned to Namin to retake a throne cruelly stolen."

"And we're to assume you're the rightful heir, then?" Baron Threstaught called. He had been leaning indolently against the wall to the left, near one of the tapestries depicting a long-gone ancestor glowing golden with magic, his hands outstretched over a kneeling populace. "Sorry to disappoint you, but there isn't anyone alive who can make that claim aside from Prince Cadell."

"Prince Cadell is dead," Carmillian announced, holding out her hands to forestall the questions immediately shouted at her. "But since he was a false prince, his death is no loss to Namin."

"And you still think you can take the throne just like that?" Threstaught sneered. He glanced at Caro briefly, and his lip curled even further.

"One hundred and twenty years ago, the heir to the throne of Namin was a princess named Cally. She had the power to see the past, present, and future, the same as her father, the king. Her older brother was jealous, selfish, and spoiled. He wanted the throne, but he could only see past and present. His power was lesser, so Cally was chosen as heir instead." Carmillian looked around the room briefly, gauging the rapt audience, before returning her gaze to Threstaught. "He killed his parents in their sleep. Despite the king of the time being able to see the future, he refused to believe the son he loved would turn so evil. When the prince went to kill his sister, she was gone, for she had seen and believed the future. And the future was clear: she had to flee, if only to ensure the future of the country she had been raised to serve. She knew the power of the royal family of Namin would wane, each subsequent generation born with less and less ability, as long as her brother's descendants remained on the throne. But she also knew one of her descendants would return to retake the stolen throne and return Namin to the greatness that once was."

Carmillian didn't look away from Threstaught, but somehow her presence had the rest of the room focused on her.

"The future is still clear," she continued after allowing for a moment of profound silence, although Caro could sense skepticism in the way some people were shaking their heads in disbelief. Carmillian let out a breath and her third eye opened, the golden glow of her magic suffusing her body with light. "The future of Namin could be great, a chance for everyone to prosper in wealth and in happiness." Her voice rang with power as well as authority, her words as suffused with her magic as her body. "But only if I am allowed to sit in this seat," she added with a wave toward the empty throne. "If you allow the false king to regain power, in five years Namin will no longer exist. The eastern lands will belong to Toval, the west will fall to tribal warfare, and the city of Svental will be nothing but rubble." The golden glow faded and her third eye closed. "I want Namin to prosper as one of the most influential countries in the world, and I promise I can ensure that happens if you'll support me along the way."

She slowly turned her head, looking at every single person assembled in the room, catching each gaze with her own. Caro knew what that felt like, as if she could look through him, see the heart of what made him, and parse all his secrets. He had felt it when she spoke to him while she was in the courtyard and Caro was using his magic to eavesdrop, and he could see the impact she was having now. Some of the courtiers bowed, others simply nodded, and even the ones that didn't move had a wide-eyed look of "oh shit." There would be no passive-aggressive backstabbing with her on the throne, and the practice of allowing the nobles to skim money and resources off the crown to pacify them was over. While that certainly panicked some people, more had the beginnings of dawning relief showing on their faces. Lowered shoulders, faint smiles, and the tight wrinkles around mouth and eyes from pinched worry beginning to fade.

Of course, these were men and women accustomed to the vagaries of the court; their first instinct was distrust. Carmillian would have to prove to them tenfold that she meant what she said, but somehow Caro didn't think that would be much of a problem for her.

Threstaught's scowl had reduced to a thoughtful frown. Caro had zero idea whether he would end up being a problem or an asset, but at the very least he no longer said anything disparaging.

"I will—" Carmillian cut herself off at the same time as Caro's magic pinged. *Danger incoming.*

Chapter Seventeen

MAGIC FLARED, YANKING Caro downward. He dropped to his knees just as an arrow passed through where his head had been, clattering harmlessly onto the floor behind him. Caro looked up, his magic still firing strong, just in time to see another arrow flying toward the dais. Except, this one was heading straight for Carmillian. Caro scrambled to dive forward, but he had fallen awkwardly and the extra second to get his feet untangled meant he was much too slow. The arrow was going to hit Carmillian and destroy Namin's last hope for survival. Gasps and screams erupted from the crowd; Caro tried to shout but found he didn't have the breath to make any noise.

However, Carmillian simply tilted her head slightly. The arrow zipped harmlessly past her ear, thudding into the throne behind her. She turned to look at the arrow, her expression completely unconcerned. When she returned her attention to the audience she let out an exasperated sigh.

"Fitting that the arrow you shot at me instead mars a symbol of your failed reign," she called out, looking in the direction from where the two arrows had been shot. "I didn't even need my magic to avoid that," she added. "And the explanation as to why is as simple as your thought process is in trying to kill me. You are a false king sitting on a stolen throne. Your magic is waning; weaker than your father's, and your heir's was weaker still. So, it follows the Triumvirè sworn to follow you will be weak as well. You trained them to drown innocents in the moat, or to push them off a tower." She grinned and her eyes were alight with viscous benevolence. "The true Triumvirè, the ones who followed the rightful queen into exile, have no such weakness."

She flicked her wrist as if shooing away a bug. Suddenly, two people appeared on the dais. Caro hadn't known they were nearby, hadn't seen them arrive, and had zero idea they had followed Carmillian's group into the throne room, but there they abruptly stood. Wearing head to toe black, with every inch of skin covered and a deep, tight-fitting hood concealing their faces, menacing was a tame way to describe them. They walked past where Caro was still sprawled, their steps completely silent as if their feet didn't touch the floor.

Caro scrambled to stand as the two people appeared to blur, and suddenly they were off the dais and halfway across the room. The crowd scampered away, leaving three people exposed. Two were in the red armor of what Caro had thought was part of the Triumvirè uniform, but their faces weren't concealed. In comparison, they looked like petulant soldiers, rather than the scary boogeymen of Namin. Both were holding cross-bows, but only one was able to reload and fire before the dark figures reached them. The third arrow thudded into the side of the dais below

Carmillian's feet.

A brief glint of silver showed, and then a spray of red as blood flew. Both red-clad bodies dropped to the ground, throats neatly cut in a stroke that, had Caro blinked, he would have missed. Then the black-clad Triumvirè turned to look at the third figure along with everyone else in the room.

The third person was in his dressing robe, same as everyone else in the room, but he had donned a cloak with a hood that concealed his face. Still, it wasn't difficult to guess who had managed to sneak in.

"You are the liar!" King Cyphus snarled, throwing his hood back defiantly to reveal his scowling face and gray-streaked blond hair. "Your ancestor abandoned this land, leaving Namin to suffer. My family has ensured this land prospered!"

"The fields are barren and the people starving," Carmillian replied, her tone scathing and her scowl fierce. "While you luxuriate in excess and murder your detractors. Namin will be a failed state by spring. And all of that is your fault, your failure as leader."

"I will see you hanged! You, and that traitor standing next to you!"

As Cyphus snarled, he was also taking small, tentative steps backward. His eyes flickered around the room, as if he was searching for a friendly face or any sort of support from those gathered. Or maybe he was searching for an escape route, Caro realized as Cyphus shuffled closer to the large doors at the other side of the room. Never mind that there were guards stationed there loyal to either Toval or to freeing Namin.

"Toval will pay for this invasion!" he continued, spit bubbling at the corners of his mouth. "I'll raze their capital and when Etoval is in ruins, Toval will bow to me too!" He suddenly spun to face the doors and started sprinting in that direction. "You'll regret this!"

The two masked Triumvirè turned to look at Carmillian, who held out a hand to stay them. With her other hand she reached into her sleeve and pulled out a small dagger. She drew her arm back, aimed, and threw.

The knife flew through the air, flashing silver as it passed through the beams of early afternoon sunlight starting to shine through the high windows in the wall to Caro's right. Heads of the onlookers turned as they followed its path. King Cyphus only got a few more steps away, and then the knife slid into his back with a meaty thud that echoed with finality. He dropped in place, like a puppet whose strings had been cut. The knife hilt glittered high and to the left of his spine, a direct hit to the heart.

"A fitting death," Carmillian murmured, although in the absolute silence of the room, everyone heard her. "He died as he lived, fleeing from his problems while whining and blaming others for his mistakes." She looked away from Cyphus's body to glance over the room again. "Right. I think we've all had far too exciting a morning. Go back to your rooms. I won't reconvene court until tomorrow at the earliest, but I will warn you now. For those of you used to taking more than your share and flouting the laws of this kingdom, your grace period to end your misdeeds is short. After my coronation, anyone caught committing any of the crimes that have beggared this nation will suffer the full consequences of the laws, which include significant fines, prison time, loss of your title, or even execution. I suggest you take some time over the next few days ensuring all your personal and business practices are compliant." She threw another glance across the room, after which Carmillian nodded, then turned sharply on her heel and headed for the secret door.

Caro was much slower to turn and follow. Wrenching his eyes away from that glittering knife and that still body was hard, far harder than Caro had ever imagined it would be. Caro had hated his father, had never identified anything redeeming about the man, and yet for some reason an ache in his chest grew the longer he looked at what was left of the man who had raised him—as poorly as that raising had been. Somewhere, hidden deeply away in the recesses of Caro's hopes and wishes, the forlorn desire that one day his father might praise him, one day Caro might be acknowledged, had somehow persisted. Now, his father was dead and with his death Caro's last dream of having a loving, welcoming family had died too.

He reached the annex and walked through the crowd to the door, which they had been waiting for him to open. He pushed the button and pulled the lever, and the door popped open. Braxton was standing on the other side. He took one look at Caro and unfolded his crossed arms, then held out his hands. Caro fell into his waiting embrace. Armor pressed against armor again, uncomfortable and in the way, and yet Braxton's warmth still penetrated. His strength held Caro up and kept the trembling bits of Caro's soul contained.

"Prince Caro, Prince Braxton, I appreciate all your help today. I will have Captain Thris guide me to the servants' hall to address them and show me to the offices of state. You both should take some time today to rest and recuperate. I will see you for breakfast tomorrow." She nodded formally to them both and then followed Thris down the passageway.

"I'll let Captain Zain and Prince Fen know too," Captain Grall added, before he also followed the group. In a few moments, Caro and Braxton were alone.

"Is there somewhere private we can go?" Braxton murmured into Caro's hair where his cheek was pressed against the top of Caro's head.

The words took a moment to penetrate before Caro nodded. "My room should be empty."

He didn't want to pull away from Braxton, but standing and hugging in the hallway wasn't an option either. Caro only stepped back enough to grip Braxton's hand, leading him down the secret passages yet again.

Caro's bedroom was down a few floors, back in the direction where Braxton's search party had been. The secret door didn't have a lock; the room wasn't nice enough to warrant one. Caro slid his fingertips into a groove and the door slid sideways into a pocket in the wall. The room itself was an inner room, so no windows, but there was very little in the way of furniture to impede Caro as he made the familiar trek across the room to the actual door where the switch to activate the mage lights was located.

With the lights on, the sparseness of the space was revealed. A small bed along one wall with a wooden box used for a side table. A set of drawers on the other wall, scratched but perfectly serviceable. And a closet that led to the shared bathing space between his room and the usually empty one next door. And that was it. No decorations, nothing to personalize it. Everything was covered in a layer of dust.

Caro dragged the blanket off the bed and took it into the hallway where he could shake it out. When he returned to the room, Caro finally found the courage to look at Braxton to gauge his reaction.

Braxton's lips were set into a frown. "I know you said your father hated you, but you're still a prince of Namin," he said, turning slowly in a circle as if he thought he might have missed something.

"I'm lucky to have this much. But I spent most of my time away from the castle for one reason or another. This is still luxury compared to camping on the ground." Caro shrugged and focused on spreading the blanket back across the bed. He turned around when he heard a thud, to see

Braxton had removed his vambraces and dropped them onto the otherwise empty top of the chest of drawers. He was working on the buckles for the armor on his chest, twisting awkwardly to reach. Caro let the blanket go and hurried over to help. Between the two of them, they soon had all the pieces of Braxton's armor off and scattered across the flat surface on top of the drawers in no time.

"Let's get yours too," Braxton said when he was down to the padded undershirt and pants worn underneath heavy armor. He didn't wait for Caro to agree, already reaching for the buckles and straps.

The second the last piece of Caro's armor was removed, Braxton wrapped his arms around Caro and hugged him close. Braxton let out a slow breath, his body relaxing beneath the fingers Caro pressed to his shoulders.

"Finally," Braxton said, laying his cheek against the top of Caro's head again.

Warmth, and the feel of Braxton's heart pounding. Skin touching skin. Caro let out his own sigh as he relaxed into the comfort of being able to actually feel Braxton again. He buried his face into Braxton's shoulder, wrapped his arms around Braxton's neck, and shamelessly clung.

"My father hated me, and I hated him," Caro forced out, his throat and chest tight. "I was glad to know we were traveling here to kill him, as terrible as that sounds. But…" He couldn't finish, his breath hitching in his throat.

Braxton turned them and practically carried Caro the two steps across the room. He sat on the edge of the bed and Caro somehow ended up in his lap, still clinging.

"My Uncle Randolph used to bring me sugar candies. He'd go out to the market and come back with his pockets full of them. When I was a kid I thought he was the coolest man in the world. He threw a coup a few years later. Killed my aunt—his sister—and came really close to killing Ayer. He planned to kill my parents as well as Fen and me, and he fled when he failed. When I found him again, you know what he said to me? 'I used to dote on you to bring you to my side. You could be my heir,' he told me as if cheap candies meant to entice a child was enough to offset the terrible things he did. And yet, after I killed him, I cried." Braxton's breath hitched and he gulped before he continued. "Try as I might, as much as I know how terrible he was, sometimes I still remember those brief moments when I thought he might be good and wish there could have been a different outcome for us all."

Caro's own tears wet Braxton's shirt where his cheek was pressed. "My brother used me as his personal practice dummy, but aside from that, ignored my existence. I felt *nothing* when he died. An almost empty sort of relief filled me, but I was also distracted by my father getting away. Seeing my father die…" he trailed off again. "I guess I did feel some sort of relief. I'll never have to look over my shoulder again, or spend every moment waiting to be murdered."

Rationalizing wasn't helping assuage the twisted sort of sadness mixed with anger roiling inside. Caro shifted, trying to press more of himself into Braxton's warmth. Braxton tightened his arms obligingly.

"You can miss the concept of someone, the idealization of what they were supposed to be, without missing the person himself," Braxton said. "If I can miss the doting uncle despite now knowing what was really under that facade, you can miss your father too."

"He didn't even try for a facade with me," Caro got out, his voice thick with tears he was struggling not to shed. "He was my father in blood only. And— And I—"

The dam burst. Caro clung to Braxton as the tears flowed. Braxton clung back, holding him close and rocking gently, and allowing Caro to mourn for what could have been, safe in the arms of what Caro knew his future would hold.

Interlude

AMA WATCHED AUNT Millie walk down the center aisle of the throne room, going between the rows and rows of seated courtiers and other important guests. While Prince Fen had returned home with the majority of the Tovalian soldiers not long after the battle cleanup ended, Prince Braxton was seated in the front row along with the handful of representatives other nearby countries had sent—mostly the ambassadors who had already been in Namin. Of course, Braxton might have remained behind more because of Prince Caro than because he was the emissary from the kingdom of Toval; Ama was fairly certain Captain Grall was going to be left behind as ambassador rather than Toval choosing Braxton. Prince Caro was standing on the dais, to the left of the priest wearing ceremonial coronation robes. Behind him was his half-sister Cybil, who had survived their father's murderous attentions by running away from home. Aunt Millie had found her working as a servant in the castle, so she hadn't gone far. To the priest's right stood Cassie, Aunt Millie's oldest child. Cassiopeia was Carmillian's heir, with the brilliant blonde hair and blue eyes of all those who inherited the magical power of the Namin throne. She had arrived without needing an invitation a few days ago along with a number of people from their home village in Toval, which was populated entirely by the descendants of those who had fled Namin all those years ago. The village wasn't empty—not everyone had been interested in returning to Namin—but Aunt Millie had plenty of support behind her.

In an unfortunate coincidence, the location of their village in Toval was almost exactly at the end of the new path Namin had been carving through the mountains toward Toval. Prince Fen had promised Aunt Millie to speak with King Aurelius about fortifying the village and turning it into a trading destination ready for the surplus of travelers who would no doubt use the better road through the Spikehorn Mountains rather than the dangerous path farther north.

All that was left was actually crowning Carmillian as queen.

Thankfully, no one had actively protested her taking control. Ama was certain there were rumblings behind the scenes, but the ruler of Namin had to have the royal magic, so the alternate options for those rumblers were limited to the three people with power currently standing on the dais. Cybill didn't have enough power to rule, Caro wasn't interested and wouldn't be given the respect the position demanded, and Cassie was perfectly happy to let her mother live a long and fruitful life before she took the throne. Ama knew there were a scant handful more people with Namin's royal magic out there, but none with any interest in sitting on a throne, nor did they have any interest in making their existence public, himself included.

"Namin has the unique domain over past, present, and future," the priest called, his voice ringing through the room. "Claimant to our throne, prove your dominion over the past!"

Aunt Millie paused in the aisle and her eyes suddenly started to glow golden as she called on her magic.

"Namin was once the continent's largest exporter of wheat and oats, before the false king stole the throne. Our fields were vast and fruitful, using techniques unique to our lands. When I am queen, I will use my dominion over the past to bring those techniques back into use so our fields return to the prosperous state of before!"

The glow faded from her eyes, and she started walking again.

"Claimant to our throne," the priest called again. "Prove your dominion over the present!"

Aunt Millie paused, now a little past halfway down the aisle, and the glow returned.

"I see starvation and desperation, children crying, and adults grieving. And I see our salvation, mere days away in a caravan sent from our friends in Toval. Grain, tubers, late autumn vegetables. Seeds to store for our spring planting. Enough that, with care, all the people of Namin may survive the coming winter and thrive with the arrival of spring."

She closed her eyes, cutting off the radiance from her magic. When she opened them again, her eyes were back to normal blue. Aunt Millie resumed walking. When she reached the foot of the three steps leading onto the dais, the priest called out again.

"Claimant to our throne, prove your dominion over the future!"

This time, Aunt Millie's third eye opened in the center of her forehead, and the flare of golden magic was so brilliant, some of those sitting in the closest seats gasped.

"I see power, and I see peace." Even Aunt Millie's voice resonated with her magic, echoing through the room like a thunderclap. "Power as one of this continent's strongest nations, able to come to any negotiation or prospective agreement from a position of strength. Peace, as we embrace our role as part of the greater whole, willing to work with others to achieve further greatness without causing pain and suffering to others."

Aunt Millie didn't use her power over the future often, Ama knew. The future was constantly changing, with minute decisions affecting major events and so many different options of what could be. She had also told him once that using it felt a bit like cheating, and that knowing when and how something would happen took the magic and mystery out of her life. That said, she did still use it when necessary.

Back when they were in the mid-construction fortress in the Spike-horn Mountains, Prince Braxton hadn't been shy asking Ama for the impossible. Once the Naminese army had agreed to work together with Toval and they jointly started planning a proper coup, Braxton had approached Ama.

"I know you're more than you appear," Braxton had said, hedging, yet still implying he understood more about Ama than he had ever even hinted at before. Braxton's expression was blank, as if Ama's secretive history really wasn't of interest to him. Ama didn't know if that was true, but at the time he had wanted to believe it. "I don't want an explanation, and I'm not looking to out your true identity," Braxton continued. "But I wonder if you might know of someone willing and able to be crowned the new king or queen of Namin. Could you go speak with them and make them an offer for the throne on behalf of Toval and Namin?"

So Ama went, sneaking out of the fortress that night and heading in the direction of his home village where Aunt Millie, Cassie, and the few others with Namin's magical royal power lived. Sometime after midnight, Ama bypassed Prince Fen's forces, who looked like they would reach the fortress by morning. Around dawn, Ama had approached another camp, this one with only one fire and two pitched tents. Thankfully, one of Aunt Millie's Triumvirè had materialized at his side before Ama could decide whether it was safe to walk past the camp or whether he needed to circumnavigate in the forest.

Aunt Millie had seen the future need: that a ruler of Namin was required and had brought only her attendants as she traveled to take her proper place. Thanks to her magic's warning, they ended up being only a few hours behind Prince Braxton and Prince Fen as the coup began.

And now, here Aunt Millie stood, about to be crowned. She didn't stop the flow of her magic this time, allowing the golden glow to suffuse her body as she ascended the three steps. She stopped in front of the priest, who nodded to her, before she turned to face the audience.

"She has learned from the past, examined the present, and used those lessons to ensure our future!" the priest called.

He lifted the royal crown of Namin off the cushioned plinth it had been resting on next to him and held it high into the air. The gold of the crown reflected the gold of Aunt Millie's magic, amplifying it until Ama was squinting to see. The priest lowered the crown slowly, placing it on her head.

"Long live Queen Carmillian Svent Namenian!"

"Long live Queen Carmillian Svent Namenian!" the audience repeated, Ama included. Everyone stood, the scraping of cloth and buttons on the seats and the thumps as people's feet took their weight the only sound for a brief moment, and then they all bowed. Namese courtiers bowed lowest, and the ambassadors from other countries bowed low as well. Prince Braxton tilted forward slightly, a bow of a foreign prince to the country's ruler. And Caro, Cybill, and Cassie all dropped to one knee, swearing themselves as fellow magic users to their new queen.

Formalities complete, a line formed from the foot of the stairs and snaking back through the throne room. Ama ignored the jockeying as courtiers fought their way toward the front to be the first to offer their congratulations, preferring to stand at the back of the room and observe.

After the greetings ended, a brief respite was planned. A light lunch followed by preparations for the celebratory ball this evening. Aunt Millie had wisely chosen not to hold a feast, since food was an issue, but Ama was perfectly okay with that. Having to sit and be formal while dining on fiddly foods sounded like torture. Not that a ball didn't sound like torture, but at least Ama could hide on the sidelines.

He was able to slip away from the throne room about a half hour later, leaving amid a large group of nobles who didn't spare him a second glance. He walked back toward his room, through the hallways he had never dared traverse openly before. If anyone asked Ama if he had ever been inside the Namin palace before, he would lie and say no. But that *was* a lie. However, the hallways appeared brighter and the air lighter than ever before as if the weight of the false king had darkened and added a heavy patina to the entire building. Having Aunt Millie on the throne and that bastard dead had returned life to the space. Still, Ama let out a small sigh of relief when he was safely inside the bedroom he had been allotted, and the door closed behind him. He didn't like being out in the open. Slinking around in the shadows was much more his style.

The servants had left the light lunch he had been promised and had laid out his far-too-fancy suit for the ball. Ama ignored the suit, greedily descending on the soup and fresh rolls left under the cloche at the small table in one corner. His room wasn't huge, a bed to the right with a small side table and a chest of drawers along the nearest wall. The other side of the room had the door to his dressing room and a bathroom shared by the adjacent room, as well as the table with two chairs, a fireplace, and a small sofa and side table in front of the fire. Not fancy, but more than sufficient for Ama's needs.

Ama had just finished eating, using a piece of the crusty bread to sop up any last liquid in the bowl, when his door flew open, and Aunt Millie sailed inside.

"There you are!" she said, closing the door much more sedately. "I know you were at the coronation, but I didn't see you afterward." She yanked him into a hug, uncaring about silly things like propriety. When she released him, she held onto his shoulders, looking at his face as if searching there would reveal some difficult answers. She finally stepped back, but only went far enough to take a seat in the other chair at the table.

"Ama, I fear you might feel as if you are being pulled in too many directions. You have loyalty to our home village, and to Toval ,which sheltered us all those years. And now new loyalties to Namin, thanks to our return to power." She paused, looking at him again, but quickly continued when Ama's purposefully blanked-out face didn't reveal whatever answer she was seeking this time. "I want you to know, who you choose to throw your own strength behind is entirely up to you. You are welcome here. You are welcome to continue working for Prince Braxton as his spy. You are welcome to quit us both and return home instead. Or, you can always find an entirely new path to take. I do not want you to feel any pressure from any of us. Understand?"

She was waiting for an answer, so Ama pulled up his courage and opened his mouth. Not that she was scary, just that he didn't really know what his answer was yet.

"I like traveling, and I enjoy what I've been doing for Prince Braxton," he said slowly, working out the words and parsing through swirling thoughts as he spoke. "And now that Namin and Toval have a strong relationship, any work I continue to do for Toval will no doubt benefit you and Namin. Besides…" He shut his mouth before the next words could escape, unwilling to say that secret aloud even if only Aunt Millie—who was privy to the secret—was around to overhear.

She nodded firmly. "Exactly. If you want my advice, I think you should continue adventuring on Prince Braxton's behalf. Have some fun for a few more years, and maybe someday you'll find whatever it is you're actually searching for."

Ama wanted to believe there was the slightest flash of magic in her eyes as she uttered those last few words, but he also didn't want to push his own wishful thinking ahead of logic. What he wanted, what he really hoped for, was completely impossible. Still, her words were sensible.

"I'll do that. At least for a few more years. I can always make a new choice later on."

"You're exactly right." Aunt Millie stood and bustled over to the door. "I need to get back before my attendants get worried. They want me to look perfect for this ghastly ball the council insisted on after I explained why we couldn't have a feast. My first task is definitely going to be replacing those fools with a competent council, but for now, we get to dance and be merry while the rest of the country starves." She scowled, but then let out a sigh as her ire faded into the acceptance of inevitability. "I'll speak with you tonight then."

She swept out as boisterously as she had entered, leaving Ama blissfully alone again. He would need to start getting ready for the ball soon, but he had a few more minutes to try to still his thoughts.

Yes, traveling on missions for Prince Braxton for a little while longer did sound nice. And it wasn't as if he had anything holding him back. No family aside from Aunt Millie, no responsibilities to anyone other than Prince Braxton, and no lover. Until something along those lines popped up, he would continue on his current path. Never mind how badly he hoped one of those three would someday manifest.

Ama laughed at his absurdity and pushed away from the table, standing to go find some water to freshen up and begin his preparations for the ball.

Someday. Sure. Maybe. But hopes and wishes were mere dreams, and dreams didn't come true for people like him. Instead, Ama would celebrate the culmination of Aunt Millie's dream, and of the dream of peace Prince Braxton had always wanted. Ama would be more than happy with that.

Epilogue

"YOU HAVE ONLY grown in strength because of what you suffered, but that doesn't mean your suffering should control you. Let it go with peace in your heart."

Kajin's final words at the end of every session didn't change, but Caro felt a strong sense of relief and comfort from them all the same. He hadn't been back at the castle in Etoval for more than five minutes before Alina cornered him and brought him here, to Kajin's office. Alina might be more than proficient at healing the body, but it took someone like Kajin to help with the mind.

Caro let out a slow breath and smiled. "I'll do my best." The sealed boxes hidden in his heart were still there, and they weren't going to go away. Pain had helped make him who he was today, and denying that it had occurred, hiding it away and pretending nothing was wrong, only helped it to control him. By acknowledging and accepting all the bad that had happened to him, Caro had blunted the edges. Although most of that success was entirely thanks to Kajin's guidance.

"I know you will," Kajin replied. He stood, his back stooped with age but plenty of strength still in him despite that. "Now, go enjoy the Frost Fair. The festivities should just be beginning, and rumor is you have a lovely man to escort you there."

Caro laughed. "I think that's long past being a rumor and is now known as fact." He had taken his lovely little throw blanket and moved into Braxton's rooms two weeks ago since he found he spent more of his time there than in his own rooms anyway. Braxton certainly hadn't objected. "He did promise to wait for me so we could go to the festival together though. I'll see you next week?"

"Of course. Go have fun!" Kajin waved Caro off, so Caro left.

Kajin's office was near the healers' ward, so it took some time for Caro to wind his way through the hallways and down to the main entrance hall for the castle. Braxton was leaning against one of the walls, waiting for him, his arms crossed and a bored expression on his face. A handful of courtiers surrounded him, and they all appeared to be talking at him, as if desperate to garner his attention. Most of the court had accepted Braxton, the perpetual bachelor, was taken, but every once in a while, those few still holding out hope that they could snare a prince crawled out of the woodwork.

Braxton caught sight of Caro walking across the room, and his expression changed, immediately lightening. He stopped leaning against the wall and said something to the crowd around him before sliding between them and striding over to meet Caro halfway.

"All set?" he asked. He leaned down, Caro tilted his head up, and their lips brushed briefly.

Caro grinned. "Let's go."

A servant brought their coats and they headed out, walking through the entrance courtyard and out into the castle bailey, and then out the main gate and onto the road leading to town.

The Frost Festival had events throughout the entire city, individual businesses and various markets hosting their own parties. However, the largest was held in the park closest to the castle walls. Karl and Shan zipped past as Caro and Braxton walked, giggling and yelling something as they ran. Prince Fen couldn't adopt them for political reasons, but Char didn't have such restrictions. By the new year in a few short months, they would be Karl and Shan Musen, orphans no longer. Although, there was apparently a third kid Caro had never met, a young girl who had been taken in by Zain.

"What are you thinking about?" Braxton asked, reaching out and taking Caro's hand so they walked together.

Caro shrugged. "Just how lucky those kids are to have a family that loves them."

"They earned that happiness," Braxton replied, looking in the direction the kids had run off to briefly before returning his attention to Caro. "Remind me to tell you that story some time." He paused, and then suddenly pulled Caro to the side of the street where they were out of the way. "You earned your happiness too, you know. And your current family is pretty awesome, if I say so myself."

"My current family?" Caro asked.

Braxton frowned at him. "I would like you to be my family. My mother already considers you like another son, and my father likes you as well. My brothers and sister love spending time with you. I hope you feel the same way about them. About me."

"I do," Caro replied, his voice barely above a whisper as he fought to suppress tears. "I really do. I just wasn't sure whether I was allowed to."

"Not just allowed. Expected. Wanted. Cherished. You are all of those things to me and to my family."

Tears formed in his eyes, Caro unable to completely hold them back anymore. Braxton ran his thumb over Caro's cheek, wiping away any evidence.

"Thank you. I really like my new family. And I love you."

Braxton grinned, bright and happy. "I love you too. Now, how about we go search this festival for some partner rings, and see whether we can beat Fen and Char to the altar!"

Caro laughed. "I'd like that." He let Braxton pull him back onto the road and into the throngs of people all heading to the festivities. He had a new family who wanted him. Friends who cared for him. And he had Braxton at his side. "Yeah. I'd really like that."

Recipes

For my readers, whenever you might need a pick-me-up of liquid gold, here's my favorite recipe for chicken soup.

Chicken Soup

INGREDIENTS

Chicken leg quarters:

Use 1 leg quarter for 3-4 servings

Use 2 leg quarters for small pot

Use 4+ leg quarters for large pot (depending on # of servings needed)

2 pkg. chicken bones

2 medium or large onions, cleaned and cut in half

6-8 carrots, peeled

2 medium or large garlic cloves, peeled

2-4 parsnips, peeled

4-6 stalks, plus all leafy tops celery

Fresh parsley, chopped

Black pepper, cracked

Dill

Salt

DIRECTIONS

1. Fill stockpot to just over half full (regardless of pot size).

2. While water is cold: add chicken bones. Rinse leg quarters, add to pot whole.

3. Bring water and chicken to a boil, then cover and turn heat down to a simmer.

4. Cook 1 hour, skimming off fat and scum regularly.

5. Clean all vegetables. Cut carrots and celery in half to fit in pot, cut parsnips in half down the middle.

6. Once pot is completely skimmed, add all vegetables. (Can leave a little fat for flavoring.)

7. Add medium to large handful of parsley, and pepper, dill, and salt (to taste). Stir. Add more spices until you can see them after stirring.

8. Cover. Simmer for two hours, stirring occasionally.

9. When soup is finished, strain through large colander into BIG bowl.

10. If serving right away, put soup back in pot to heat. Cut up cooked carrot, parsnip, and chicken and add to pot.

11. If not serving right away, set aside to cool. Store broth, vegetables, and chicken in three separate bowls. (Throw away bones and skin, but keep the chicken.).

NOTES AND VARIATIONS:
• Vegetable amounts depend on size of pot.

- Kosher chicken will be saltier, so reduce amount of salt added.
- If chicken bones are not available, consider increasing bone-in chicken amount or add a half dozen wings.
- Kosher chicken will likely have feathers; allow additional time for cleaning.
- Soup can be frozen. Freeze broth separately from vegetables and chicken.
- Chicken makes for great chicken salad!

About the Author

When Mell Eight was in high school, she discovered dragons. Beautiful, wondrous creatures that took her on epic adventures both to faraway lands and on journeys of the heart. Mell wanted to create dragons of her own, so she put pen to paper. Mell Eight is now known for her own soaring dragons, as well as for other wonderful characters dancing across the pages of her books. While she mostly writes paranormal or fantasy stories, she has been seen exploring the real world once or twice.

Facebook

www.facebook.com/MellEightFiction

Twitter

www.x.com/MellEight

Website

www.melleightfiction.weebly.com

BlueSky

bsky.app/profile/melleight.bsky.social

Instagram

www.instagram.com/mell_eight

Threads

www.threads.net/mell_eight

Other NineStar books by this author

Princes of Toval Series

The Chef

Witch's Circle Series

Coven

Hunter

Witch

Ge-Mi Series

Ge-Mi, Part One

Ge-Mi, Part Two

Oracle Series

The Oracle's Flame

The Oracle's Hatchling

The Oracle's Golem

The Oracle's Sprite

The Oracle's Prophecy

The Oracle's Current

Supernatural Consultant Series

Dragon Consultant

Dragon Deception

Dragon Dilemma

Dragon Detective

Dragon Soldier

Dragon Adventures

Dragon Lesson

Out of Underhill Series

Kelpie Blue

If a Butterfly Don't Fly

Magnified Series

Magnified

Justified

Dragon's Hoard Series

Finding the Wolf

Breaking the Shackles

Stealing the Dragon

Melting the Ice Witch

Road to… Series

Road to Revenge

Road to Home

Wizard Wars Series

Ground of Insurrection

Ground of Resurrection

Standalone Books

Elemental Ride

A Little Fairy Dust

Wounded Alpha

The Coup and the Prince

Space Stars

Water's Price

Twin Elements

Soul Bond

Gifting a Dragon's Heart

www.ninestarpress.com

www.facebook.com/ninestarpress

www.facebook.com/groups/NineStarNiche

www.twitter.com/ninestarpress

www.instagram.com/ninestarpress

bsky.app/profile/ninestarpress.bsky.social

www.threads.net/@ninestarpress

www.ingramcontent.com/pod-product-compliance
Lightning Source LLC
Chambersburg PA
CBHW071527120726
47907CB00013B/1246